A Burning Hope

by

Mathias G. B. Colwell

Published by
Melange Books, LLC
White Bear Lake, MN 55110
www.melange-books.com

Cover Art by Stephanie Flint

For Baby, the newest member of the family.

Chapter One

"Pay attention, you mangy bastard."

Aerick flicked a grin at Maeze as he began untying the skiff from its position on the dock. The words didn't hurt Maeze. That was just the way Maeze's partner spoke, and the smile said he wasn't serious. Aerick continued. "I'm sure not going to do all the work for you today." Aerick spoke like a commoner, without clear enunciation, squishing words and syllables together and at times even omitting certain sounds when he chose.

The Fortress rose firmly and resolutely behind Maeze. A circular structure, built to mimic the island upon which it sat, the Fortress was far from pretty. The architecture appeared only half finished in terms of its original conception. Four towers, one each at the north, south, west, and east side of the island, stood prominently, made of harsh stone and stained dark over the years. They had obviously been constructed first as the architects of past times began building this haven from the world. However, it was clear that the designers of the Fortress had fallen short of their expectations for materials. The northern wall was built of the same grim granite as the tower turrets, yet the other three quarters of the wall were a hodgepodge of tightly fitted logs. The northern ramparts of stone changed from one step to the next, making way for the lumber constructed walls that followed. From the midst of the chinked log walls just slightly shorter than the northern, stone ramparts, the towers would emerge, a stark contrast of stone to the logs that surrounded it.

Maeze quit staring at the Fortress standing grimly behind him and untied his end of the skiff. He rocked the sturdy little craft with one boot to test its merit. It wobbled on the water and dirty, brown liquid oozed in from the many tiny leaks around its hull, but it was firm in its ability to stay afloat and to keep the majority of the marsh water out.

"She's fen worthy," Aerick stated as he watched Maeze tip and push the skiff, testing it with one foot while keeping the other foot planted firmly on the dock.

Maeze grunted noncommittally as he thought of what lurked beneath the surface of the water. "She better be. Our lives depend on it." The comment brought a bitter twist to his partner's mouth and Aerick didn't speak again until they had cleared the tiny harbor on the south side of the Fortress where the Slayers' Docks were located.

As he and his partner rowed into the marsh and away from the Slayers' Docks—docks named for the working class fighters who departed from them—Maeze thought about how much he hated leaving the Fortress. The marsh surrounding the island held no joy for one such as him, a Slayer. Leaving the Fortress to do his daily work of protecting the settlement was hardly enjoyable. Being a Slayer meant a person had been forcefully recruited into a lifetime sentence in the lowest position in the Fortress' fighting force, which came with extreme danger and risk.

Maeze hated returning to the Fortress as well. He pretty much just hated the Fortress. In a way, he supposed that he hated the world around him in general. It was a bleak, unforgiving place from which he and his fellow man were forced to scrape a miserable existence. Well, all but the Ruling Council that was. Those few who maintained power and influence were afforded certain luxuries that others were not. Maeze wondered bitterly if he would be in his current predicament if he had been born into one of those families. Of course he wouldn't. The thought was immediate and filled with the sour taste of truth. The poor broke the law, not the rich. Oh, the rich were criminals too, their cruelty was unquestioned in Maeze's mind, yet they created the rules and could mold them any way they pleased, erecting a world where they could continue to exploit those less powerful than they.

They rowed slowly, gradually, for an hour, taking turns at the oars along the way. They had no destination in mind. There was no rush. Hell would come to them, they didn't have to find it.

Fens slid by slowly on either side. Dark, brown water, so murky the end of the oars disappeared when submerged, even just below the surface. So dark that barely a glimmer of reflection could be seen, even if a person peered into it. A ripple stirred the calm surface of the pool to Maeze's right, and both he and Aerick jumped, slightly startled, and placed a hand on their weapons as they let the oars of the skiff rest. Something rose in the midst of the ripple and Aerick sighed audibly as he saw it was just a fish. He was still new at this. Not like Maeze.

Maeze's hand gripped his flanged mace tightly even as the fear caused by the noise of the fish ebbed and silence resumed dominion of their surroundings. The boat drifted lazily, caught in a small bog swirl, those random currents that eddied through the swamp all around them, making their way in and around the humps of floating vegetation and the few solid mounds of earth that punctuated the marsh.

Such was the marsh. Small currents that could carry you anywhere and everywhere, as long as you didn't want to go any place in particular. Such was the world really. Because the marsh was the world and the world was the marsh. There was nothing in this forsaken land other than fen and bog. This was all there was, just endless dark water, vegetation, hummocks, and the occasional stunted tree for as far as the eye could see. Even farther.

Maeze and Aerick let the skiff drift on the bog swirl. They had nowhere they needed to be. Come dark they would just make sure they were back to the Fortress. That was all a Slayer really did; nearly every day they spent out on the water, waiting to kill or be killed, and by nightfall they were back within the protective, oppressive walls of the Fortress.

He fingered his weapon, as Aerick balanced the oars on the edges of the boat. His partner, not rowing any longer, instead stared moodily out over the sinister, brackish water. Maeze studied his mace, the weapon he had carried for three years now. He had come to know every inch of its surface, every nick, every scratch. The wooden handle was worn smooth from many years of use, even before it had found its way into Maeze's possession. Simply fashioned, the haft was stained dark from the endless amount of marsh water that had splashed on its surface or been soaked up from filthy hands gripping it. The haft ended in a heavy metal ball covered in sharp metal spikes, firm enough that with a powerful swing, you could crush a hole in a skull or put one of its sharp spikes in a man's heart. Or any other creature for that matter, Maeze reflected grimly. Men were the least of his concerns.

As if to punctuate that thought, a white shape bobbed to the surface and Maeze leaped into instant action swinging his mace downward with all his might, into the swamp water and directly at the object. With a tremendous splash of water from the swing, a

4

flimsy, pale stick floated disconsolately on the surface of the mucky water. It had probably drifted free of a watery prison somewhere deep beneath the surface and had arisen here.

Maeze shook from the rush of adrenaline caused by his instant and defensive action. Aerick stood with his short sword gripped fearfully in his thin hands.

"Well?" Aerick breathed the question shakily.

"False alarm," Maeze said in response, trying to muster his calm and courage. Courage was hard to find these days.

"By the Forgotten Gods," Maeze's partner cursed, "you scared the wits out of me!" Forgotten Gods. Deities from long ago, barely remembered, and spoken of in hardly more than whispers around a hearth. It was an old saying, Maeze thought as he apologized to his inexperienced companion. There was not much new about the world, he realized. Old Fortress, old, stagnant water, old land, forgotten dead, Forgotten Gods.

Everything was old and forgotten these days. Even magic was almost gone from the world, forgotten and lost to the race of men. All except the Binding. The magic of the Binding was old and powerful, but it was steeped in hopelessness, steeped in the desperation of generations. It was strong, yes, but it was dirty magic. Slave magic. Reserved to forcefully bind the criminals and common men to a lifetime of horror, making them Slayers and slaves to battle. Maeze cleared his throat of phlegm and spat it over the side of the boat to float filmy white on the surface of the swamp.

"Sorry," Maeze muttered to Aerick. His partner smiled back at him nervously.

"It's ok, you mutt." Aerick's eyes flicked across the water nervously, searching for the appearance of any other white shape, rather than the pale stick that had startled them into action. "You're an old-timer," he winked at Maeze, "and bound to be a bit more fidgety than a young buck like me."

Maeze faked a laugh for his partner's benefit. It was true; he was older than Aerick in years, but even more so in experience. It was the length of time Maeze had been a Slayer to which Aerick had referred in his jest. Maeze had been a Slayer for over three years now, nearly an eternity compared to most other Slayers. Many Slayers didn't survive their first month, let alone a first week on the job. His partner, Aerick, was still fresh from a filthy jail cell, and the reasonably clean air of the swamp, punctuated only occasionally by a sulfur filled breeze from the underground hot springs bubbling up in random locations, was still better than from where he had come. The life of a Slayer still felt like freedom to Aerick, it still felt like a second chance to him. Maeze, however, knew the bitter reality. There were no second chances in this world, the Ruling Council saw to that. They governed the Fortress with an iron fist and martial law. The life of a Slayer was just another form of incarceration. It was a slow death, a life of horror.

"You ever think about what it might have been like before the last Surge, Aerick?" Maeze kept a steady eye on his surroundings as he spoke. One didn't lose focus outside the walls of the Fortress. It was always a good idea to keep one eye on the water.

"It was nearly fifty years ago, partner." Aerick still twiddled his sword idly in his hands, the oars hanging listlessly from their oarlocks. "Why concern yourself with the ancient past?"

"Ancient? Fifty years is hardly ancient."

"Well," Aerick rebutted, "I don't know of anybody older than forty, except maybe on the Ruling Council, but the governors don't count in conversations such as these." He had a point, Maeze supposed. Fifty years was certainly a long time in this world.

Maeze decided not to press the question further. He didn't want to argue with Aerick. Maeze had actually broken his own personal rule. He liked his partner and didn't want to have a disagreement. In his three years as a slayer he had realized it was never good to like your partner. Trust, confidence, belief, all those emotions were good. You had to trust the man fighting next to you, fighting for you. But becoming friends with your partner was always a bad idea. It was never a good idea to become friends with a person you might be forced to kill. Maeze had crossed that line in the weeks since he had gained a new scar on his chest during his and Aerick's Binding, and he was not entirely certain how to escape his current predicament.

Aerick, however, didn't seem ready to end the discussion. "Why are you asking?"

Maeze shrugged neutrally. "Just a thought. I wonder what it would have been like before all this." He waved his hand at himself and his partner, as he answered in his commoner speech, which was just as thick as Aerick's.

"Before the Slayers?" Aerick asked.

Maeze nodded. "Yah. Before this. Us. And..." Now Maeze paused, unsure if he really wanted to go on. He decided he would and pushed on in a self-conscious rush. "And, just in general. Like what else is out there?" He indicated the horizons all around them in a circle, with one sweeping gesture of his arm.

Aerick shook his head in sour amusement. "There is nothing

else. This is all there is. The Fortress. The Cells. Our weapons." Maeze's partner shook his sword to emphasize his point and toed the spiked ball at the end of Maeze's flanged mace with his boot as well. "Might as well just accept it."

"What if it isn't, what if I can't?" Maeze asked in response, uncharacteristically philosophical and honest, even with himself. "You know I saw a pile of ruined stones once when I was in my first year as a Slayer," he mused thoughtfully to Aerick. "It was nearly the end of the week and my partner and I were completely under the Quota. We drifted for almost a full day west trying to fulfill the requirements when I saw the ruins," Maeze remembered.

Aerick shook his shortly cropped, black-haired head. "It's useless to think of such things. Just be glad you're outside of a jail cell right now. That's blessing enough. Besides, what would you do, just go? Where would you go? There is nothing outside of the Fortress. There never has been and there never will be."

Maeze dropped the discussion. He had admitted to himself that his skinny, black-haired partner was pleasant to be around most of the time, but he just didn't think very much. Aerick was willing to eat whatever was fed to him. Literally and figuratively.

Maeze looked at the still brown surface of the water as the boat drifted into a silent pond-sized pool in the marsh. The light of mid-morning splashed in brilliant rays upon the still water, and he almost caught a reflection in the surface. Almost. Even with the sunlight, it was still too dark to see his face clearly. Maeze had seen his own true reflection once, however. He had bedded a girl a few months back that had possessed a shard of mirror. The girl had pressed the shard of mirror into the earthen wall of her dugout basement room beneath the East Quarter tavern. She had been a barmaid. How she had come to possess such a treasure he didn't know. But Maeze remembered the shard of mirror more than the night he had spent with her. It was the only time in his life when he had seen his reflection. The moment would forever be frozen in his mind. Maeze remembered gazing into the broken piece of mirror and seeing a sallow, underfed face looking back at him. His brown hair had been lank and greasy from lack of washing and had been slicked back to fall behind his ears half way to his shoulders. Brown eyes had stared back at him, as he'd looked at his own unshaven face, the stubble a few days grown and crooked teeth set against pale, dirty skin. It was a poor man's face. Maeze was, after all, a poor man. It had not been the face of one of the upper class.

"Come on, let's row for a bit," Aerick said, grabbing the oars. "We've had no luck yet today." There was an intensity in Aerick's face as he proposed a change of location. Maeze understood; he had been living with that same burden for three years. He wasn't sure if he would refer to what they were lacking as *luck*, however. They were Slayers. Whether they met the Quota or not, luck had deserted them long ago. It had deserted the world.

Aerick paddled them gradually southeast, fighting an idle current, a bog swirl trying to drag their little skiff backwards. Maeze picked up the long pole lying prostrate in the skiff and began poling the ground far beneath the water to aid his partners paddling. They held their course, with Aerick rowing, Maeze poling, until perhaps another hour had passed. The Fortress was the only thing on the horizon to break up the monotony of the marshland. Other than that bleak object of human construction to the north, there was nothing man made to punctuate the scenery. Rushes, some taller than a man, protruded up from the murky water. Other, smaller weeds grew in among the rushes or created little floating islands upon which a man could lay down for a damp nap. If he wanted to tempt fate that was. It was never a good idea to sleep outside the Fortress.

The tension rose as they searched for a new location. Maeze could see the anxiety begin to form on the face of his usually optimistic friend. Aerick's forehead began to bead with sweat from worry. He paddled harder, splashing and slopping water over the edges of the boat, soaking their feet.

"Calm down." Maeze put a hand on his partner's forearm to stop his paddling. "Let's just find us something solid to stand on and then we'll go from there."

Aerick inhaled deeply, struggling to silence his nerves. Finally he nodded to Maeze and breathed again, a long sigh, almost a moan of fear as he dipped the oars back into the swamp water with a touch more control than before.

"There, that looks pretty sturdy," Aerick exclaimed quietly, pointing with an oar, indicating a hummock of island which appeared to be anchored down below the water.

"Bring us around then," Maeze stood up in the wobbly skiff as they approached the small hump of land. As they drew near enough to touch it, Maeze lifted one leg over the side and kicked the hummock expertly. It stayed firm. He kicked it again and again. Still it did not move.

"Looks like it's solid," he murmured to Aerick. Onc could never be too sure. Some of the islands were really nothing more than floating vegetation, which over the years had collected seeds and grown even more plants on top. It lent many of these islands the look of stability, yet once upon their surface the truth was quickly surmised. Many of the floating islands were large enough to hold your weight but not much else. Moving around often tipped them and sent the occupant sprawling into the fetid water of the surrounding fens. No man wanted to be in the water. Chill as the grave, the cold marshy water iced a man's nerve and courage. Maeze had seen even the bravest of men falter and turn to children when the swamp depths closed over their head. Listening to a full-grown soldier scream in panic was something you didn't forget.

Maeze stepped across the side of the skiff and onto the solid ground of the small hummock. It was no more than ten feet from one end to the other lengthwise and the same across. The island was indeed sturdy and solid, since he could walk and stamp his feet all he liked with no movement of the earth beneath him. Aerick stepped onto the sodden ground of the hummock and jabbed the anchor spike into the ground to moor the skiff. The rope connecting the anchor spike to the skiff was covered with old, dried algae, the plants crusted onto the line from previous use.

"Well, what do we do now?" Aerick asked nervously. Maeze felt pity for him. He had hardly ever been low on his Quota since joining and becoming Maeze's partner and he clearly didn't feel confident at all. If you were a Slayer for long enough, eventually you ran into many such situations like this.

"Give me your hand," Maeze responded in answer. Aerick trustingly reached out and placed his hand firmly in Maeze's grasp. In a quick motion, he sliced a shallow cut on Aerick's palm, and then did the same to his own. His partner swore in a pained voice, clutching his hand to his chest.

"Did you have to do it so hard," he complained to Maeze.

Maeze ignored the question. "Come on now. Squeeze the blood out."

Maeze watched as his partner pumped his hand a few times to really get the blood moving. "No, not here," Maeze exclaimed in frustration, watching the blood fall onto the small island. "Hold your hand over the water. Let the blood drip into the marsh water. It does us no good if we waste the blood on the soil." Amateur. Aerick should be more accustomed to this by now. It was not the first time either one of then had been bled in order to attract their targets.

"Sorry," Aerick muttered. "It just hurts. I wasn't thinking straight."

"Forget about it. You know the wound will go away soon enough. Well, provided they come." Maeze added the last bit as an afterthought. Aerick nodded his understanding and allowed his bright, red blood to drip freely into the muddy water near the edge of the small island, mimicking Maeze who was doing the same thing. Their blood hit the dark water and formed a strange looking slick, almost like oil.

The world around them was brown as always. Dim water, tan rushes, the dark brown wood of the Fortress far to the north on the horizon; the earth beneath their feet matched the brown of the boat and their clothes also. Everything was dull in this world. The marsh was all there was and it permeated everything. The only exceptions were the tiny wisps of mist that danced their way through the air. They were not thick enough to obstruct anything from view. Indeed the solemn silhouette of the Fortress hours to the north was clear to their vision. Yet the wisps managed to add the only light quality, the sole, bright attribute, to this dark and sinister landscape. Sunlight shone from above and glanced through the wisps of mist reflecting through the droplets of water in the air and scattering everywhere around. Maeze thought of how it was the only beauty to be seen today.

They wrapped their hands in a quick bandage and then waited in silence for a few minutes, watching the marsh breezes stir the various clusters of reeds and rushes. Minutes turned into another hour and the midday sun shone high over top of them, its warmth, normally a comfort against the chill of the swamp, was today only another reminder of their race against time.

Fear began to show in Aerick's eyes as he clutched his cut hand to his chest. Maeze knew his eyes probably looked the same as his partner's. The fear never left, even after years as a Slayer. It was always there, it's cold, deathly hands clamping chill fingers around your belly. Maeze could feel his body tightening up with worry. He felt anxious that they would run out of time today and miss their Quota—the number of kills required of a Slayer partnership each week—and yet also feared the circumstances that would allow them to fulfill it. Being far short of the Quota at the end of a weekly cycle was a terrifying process all around. On the one hand a Slayer needed to get his kills to stay alive, but on the other hand facing the dangerous creatures he was required to kill in order to protect the people of the Fortress, could very easily cost him his life.

Two more hours passed and the sun began to sink slowly toward the western horizon. It was only early afternoon but Maeze knew they couldn't afford to wait much longer.

"We'll never be able to pay the Death Tax when we get back to the Fortress tonight, unless we do something now." Maeze's words were calm and assured, masking the fear writhing in the pit of his stomach. He directed a steady stare at Aerick. Maeze's partner was only a few months old as a Slayer and he hadn't yet faced a day like today. Aerick would face many more such ones as this in his future as a Slayer. If he survived, that was.

Finally Aerick nodded his head in acceptance. "Let's just get it over with. Do you have a coin?"

Maeze nodded he did. It wasn't actually money. It was a flat, rounded chip of wood with a face painted on either side, used for situations of chance. On one side was the face of the High Magistrate, the leading member of the Ruling Council, and on the other was the face of the Grand Investigator. It was a chip used for flipping and deciding outcomes.

"You want to be the investigator or the magistrate?" Maeze let his partner decide.

Aerick swallowed back his fright. Sometimes Maeze forgot that he was still fairly young, not more than twenty years of age compared to Maeze's thirty years.

Aerick shrugged his shoulders glumly. "Magistrate, I guess. Not that it really matters." It didn't, he was right. But Maeze wanted to be polite. He had finally admitted to liking his partner, even against all his common sense. It was days like today when he knew it for true. Moments like right now, when they were flipping a coin to decide who had the honor of receiving a sword in the gut. It was never a good idea to make friends with a partner you might be forced to kill.

Maeze offered the coin to his partner out of courtesy, once again trying to be polite. Even if it went against his common sense, he wouldn't change his actions now. He already liked him and at this point, acting rude wouldn't make what happened next any easier. Aerick shook his head and motioned for Maeze to flip it.

The coin released up into the air from Maeze's flipping thumb, rotating end over end in a mesmerizing pattern. Even though this was hardly his first time flicking a coin to see who lived, he still felt the stirrings of terror in his heart. He had been on either end of the coin in the past. In some instances he had received his wounds and then been healed, rising from a state of near death. At other times he'd been required to deliver a potentially killing wound to his partner and then fight for both their lives. It was a confusing circumstance and if it weren't for the slave magic of the Binding it wouldn't be possible.

Maeze caught the coin as it dropped and then smacked it over onto the back of his hand, looking at the face staring up at them.

"Magistrate," Aerick breathed miserably. Almost, almost, Maeze offered to switch with his partner. But no. He didn't like the lad that much. Where were his senses going?

"Ill luck, Aerick," Maeze commiserated with his partner. "I'll do my best to make sure you make it through. Alright?"

Aerick nodded. "I know you will. You're the best partner one could ask for. I'd heard such horror stories before I became a Slayer, tales of partners butchering their pair in response to a bad toss of the coin, dicing them up nearly beyond the point of resurrection. It terrified me." Aerick gulped. "But you, you've been a good one."

"Don't get all sentimental on me, Aerick," Maeze said gruffly. "Odds are you'll be back from the brink of death and in the Fortress tonight." *I hope*, he thought silently. Even three years of life as a Slayer hadn't turned Maeze into a warrior. The hell about to break loose after he gutted his partner was by no means easy to survive, even if you were hale enough to fight. If he was lucky, Maeze would make it home tonight, but it would take a considerably larger amount of fortune for the same to be said of Aerick. Maeze spat as he thought. But that was the Ruling Council for you. They made damn certain that reaching the end of the week short on the required Death Tax to meet the Quota was worse than dying for a Slayer.

The sun sank a little bit lower. "Ready?" Maeze asked quietly. "It's better for both of us if this doesn't happen in the dark. And you know how quickly twilight arrives on the water." He felt slightly insensitive to rush his partner, his friend, he admitted reluctantly. Yet, there was no getting around it.

Aerick understood. He forced a light laugh. "Yes, it certainly will be better for me if you can see what you're fighting." Maeze nodded at his friend's bravado.

"Good lad."

"Let's get this over with," Aerick said roughly, the time for joking aside. He handed Maeze his short sword and then squared off in front of him, bracing himself against the thrust he knew would come, eyes shut tightly.

"Aerick, take off your shirt. No reason to slice up a good tunic. You'll be glad of it when this is all over and done." Maeze said gently.

Aerick opened his squinting eyes and sighed. "Right." He stripped off his shirt then squared off again with Maeze as he tossed the tunic on the ground beside him.

Maeze saw that Aerick had no scars on his stomach to show yet. That would change. Maeze himself possessed three such scars on his own stomach, evidence of the same brutal savagery he was about to inflict upon his friend. An average of one each year, he thought grimly. Maeze didn't know if he should consider those odds good or bad. He supposed if he was a better fighter or a more successful hunter, then it might not be necessary. If he'd been more skilled, then maybe he wouldn't have ever fallen short of Quota at the end of a week. But most Slayers didn't come from soldier backgrounds. Most were simple criminals, unschooled in the arts of a war into which they were thrust. Maeze had been no different. He had never been a soldier even though it paid well to be one. But if he had to do it over again, he would have done it that way, been a normal soldier. Standing behind the ramparts of the Fortress, defending it against attackers was better than floating around the swamp in a rickety skiff, waiting for hell to find you. Anything was better than being a Slayer. Unfortunately, he had not always considered it so. He had passed up the opportunity to be a soldier, instead trying to scrape a living as a handyman, doing odd jobs, whatever labor he could find. He had turned to petty crime as soon as his stomach was empty. Pickpocketing, thieving a loaf of bread here or a mug of ale there off a stranger's tavern table. Then came the fateful day when he had been caught and thrown into the dank cell, deep beneath the Fortress. The Grand Investigator had informed him of his options; live out his life as a prisoner or become a Slayer. It had seemed an obvious choice at the time. Now, Maeze wasn't so certain. Even a life of imprisonment might be better than the constant state of fear in which a Slayer lived. Well, maybe not. Maeze was of two minds about that, vacillating back and forth depending on the day. Today, with the frenzy ahead of him, he felt certain he would prefer a cell to what he was about to face.

"Ready?" Maeze asked again.

"Just do it already," Aerick muttered between clenched teeth, the young man's pale, stomach muscles contracting as he tightened them in terror against the pain he knew would come, eyes still closed.

"Relax your stomach muscles, it will hurt less." Maeze advised, cocking his arms back behind him as he prepared to thrust with the sword.

Aerick nodded again in agreement and noticeably relaxed his abdomen for a moment. Without pausing to give his partner another chance to tighten up again in fear, Maeze rammed the point of the sword hard into his friend's belly, jamming the tip all the way out the other side. A froth of blood poured from his partner's mouth as he removed Aerick's blade from the boy's own body.

Aerick was about to collapse as Maeze grabbed him to steady him. Maeze led him toward the swamp and dunked him under the murky, brown water, bits and pieces of vegetation and muck clinging to Aerick's bare torso. Blood flowed freely into the water, mingling red with brown until it created a dark soupy mixture.

"I'm sorry, Aerick, you and I both know it's the only way. We need enough blood to attract more than just a few of the bastards, and slicing our hands just wasn't going to bring enough of them to us in the little amount of daylight we have left. The Ritual Wound was the only option." Maeze apologized to his partner as he propped his friend up along the muddy bank of the small island. Blood oozed from the wound and continued to run down into the water. Good. The sooner this was over the better.

Aerick's eyes were cloudy with the shock of his first ever, potentially mortal wound. Potentially mortal because the slave magic of the Binding did have its uses after all. A Slayer was not completely without his tricks. Aerick seemed to nod his understanding to Maeze's apology but Maeze couldn't be certain if Aerick really heard him. Maeze shoved the hilt of his partner's sword into the dying young man's hand. Aerick would need his weapon if things went well.

Maeze stood up and clasped his own weapon tightly in his

hand, the leather grip on the haft of the flanged mace a familiar comfort as he waited for what he hoped and also feared would come. All there was to do now was wait. It wouldn't be long.

Sure enough, within ten minutes, they had arrived.

Fresh blood from a mortal wound called them as surely as the dawn beckoned morning. The more blood the better, especially the blood of someone dying, such as Aerick. The blood of the dying mixing into the eddies and bog swirls of the marsh attracted them like flies to a dead carcass. Maeze saw a white hand reach up from the depths of the dark brown water and grasp the now unconscious Aerick's leg, in order to drag him fully into the marsh.

Banelings.

Hell had arrived.

Maeze reacted immediately. He dragged his fallen friend up from the water's edge and laid him to rest in the center of the small island. Maeze's partner was far from safe, but it was better near the center of the hummock of land than at the water's edge.

With urgency fueled by terror, Maeze flung himself from the body of his unconscious, dying comrade back towards the edge of the marsh. Fen creatures boiled beneath the murky surface. Baneling arms and legs emerged, pale and pallid from the dark water. White humanoid heads emerged as well, with milky eyes and toothless mouths. They emitted keening wails and gurgling barks as their pure white eyes searched for prey.

Maeze, his heart constricted with fear, jumped into the shallow water up to his knees. He felt the firm grasp of their bleached hands clasping his ankles, struggling to pull him into the deep water. He smashed to his left and right with the flanged mace, the spikes of his weapon biting deeply into skulls and faces.

Banelings moaned in agony but they came on in greater numbers, boiling up from the depths of the bog surrounding the island. They advanced on Maeze, at least ten in number, some of them oozing milky, white blood from the gashes his mace had left on their bodies. Creatures of the swamp, humanoid in form, they were almost entirely white, pale, and grubby, with the droplets and sheets of mucky water running down their bodies as they emerged from the fens and laid claim to the island.

Maeze fought the urge to scream. It didn't work. His own wail of fright mixed with the keening, moaning noises of his adversaries. Fear or not, his life depended on their deaths. Maeze was a Slayer. Perhaps not a good one, but he had survived three years. That had to mean something. He flung himself back into the fray with a fearful desperation. Swinging his mace with all his might, he prayed to the Forgotten Gods that he would survive yet another day at his job.

Bones crunched, webbed fingers were crushed on their white hands as he swung his mace and wounded the beasts of the deep swamp coming to drink his blood. Crying tears of fright and at the same time screaming his bitter rage at being a Slayer, he fought for his life and the life of his friend.

Two Banelings dropped, their heads demolished by the erratic yet desperation fueled power of his blows. Their milky blood oozed out and mixed with the dirty water creating a light brown substance. Another two Banelings stumbled toward him and three more circled around behind him. One of the remaining Banelings saw Aerick lying unconscious on the ground and shambled over to approach the body. There was nothing Maeze could do for his friend at the moment. Hopefully, the lone Baneling wouldn't do too much damage to his partner.

Maeze swung his mace wildly, catching a Baneling in the shoulder. It groaned an injured noise and backed off while the other four attacked at once. The creatures did not move with any dangerous speed. They shambled and dragged their humanoid bodies, more accustomed to swimming than walking. Yet they approached inexorably. Death was the only thing that stopped them, their advance continued. They resembled the pale, white husks of humans, the shells of men. Maeze knew not where they came from and didn't care to know. He fought desperately. He was grateful, once again, for a weapon whose use required little skill or accuracy. His flanged mace was really just a fancy club with spikes. The spikes bit deeply into the skin of his enemies and the firm metal ball at the end provided the force of impact to shatter skulls and break bones. Maeze swung the mace wildly, in terror, and felt it crunch into the shuffling bodies of Banelings. One grabbed him from behind and started mouthing his neck as if searching, tasting for blood that was not there. Maeze didn't know how well they could see with their pure white eyes, he only knew they didn't think like humans. They thought of food and food alone. Blood. They drank from the open wounds of living and dead men alike.

Maeze lashed out at the two Banelings to his right, breaking an arm with one blow and spiking an eye with the other. He felt the Baneling on his back constricting its arms and legs around him. Panic welled within Maeze and he shook and flailed until the creature on his back fell off with a crash into the weeds and muck behind him.

He hazarded a glance at his partner. The Baneling who had found him was still approaching the body. Apparently not much time had elapsed since the fight began, but to Maeze it felt like hours. When your life was in danger, time passed differently. Maeze noticed that with each Baneling he killed, the gaping wound in Aerick's stomach began to shrink. Blood flowed less freely from the injury, and his partner's breathing sped up and increased until he was almost breathing naturally.

Hope flared in Maeze's breast. Five Banelings dead and his friend was improving. The Binding magic was such that with every Baneling killed by a Slayer's partner, the injured Slayer healed and mended their body. It was the old magic, ancient ties of binding. Slave magic. But it would keep them both alive today if Maeze could just fight harder.

He swung his attention back to the remaining Banelings, attacking the one about to feed on his partner. Maeze clubbed the would-be feeder senseless, seeing it drop to the turf. Dead he hoped. He was not a good fighter, but he had fought desperately at other times before today. With a scream of wild abandon he charged directly into the mass of Banelings, forcing them back toward the water's edge. Maeze swung his mace with as much force and precision as he could, cracking white, grubby bodies, bashing the hands hoping to cling to him and pull him into a watery grave. The battle ended up in the shallows of the marsh, and Maeze fought the swamp demons, with the brown, almost black, water splashing up to soak his tunic and breeches with a chill he knew would not quickly recede.

Somehow, against the odds, he killed them. He fought his hardest. For the first time ever, he fought on behalf of a friend as well as his own life. Never before had a Slayer been his comrade the way Aerick was. A sharp pain stung his arm and Maeze saw a cut forming on his forearm where one of the creatures had used a solitary claw to inflict the wound. The beast bent its head to drink from the wound before even attempting to kill him and Maeze nearly decapitated it with a powerful swing of his mace.

The lone claws on either forefinger of the Banelings were the only sharp implements on their bodies. Having no teeth, they would often lick the blood from a body or cup a steady flow in their hands from which to drink, instead of biting their victims with their toothless mouths. But the narrow nails protruding from the tips of the forefingers of each Baneling were perfectly crafted to open throats and slit veins in wrists and arms just for the purpose of feeding. Those forefingers were the only fingers not attached by webbing to the others. Free from web and with the claw, they could be deadly.

Numbers usually won out for Banelings, but with a roar, Maeze killed another in a last ditch attempt to fend one off from grappling him to the ground. He chanced another look behind him and saw that Aerick was on the mend for good now, his wound healed and his groggy eyes regaining focus.

"Hurry!" Maeze screeched at his friend anxiously. If the Banelings realized how much blood was still floating in the water then Maeze and Aerick would be in serious trouble. They had used the blood as bait to lure the creatures in; it was the whole purpose of why he had stabbed Aerick. But it was dangerous to actually allow them time to drink it. A Baneling changed when it drank enough blood. A Baneling in a blood-frenzy was a totally different beast to try and kill than one that was not.

Aerick shook the last vestiges of unconsciousness from his head and his fingers grasped the sword, which Maeze had conveniently placed in his hand earlier. He lurched to his feet and joined the fight.

Maeze's partner was no warrior either, but neither were the

Banelings. The creatures didn't think they just surged forward in numbers, wanting the precious red flow of blood from a human's body. Aerick sheered through two of them with a wild and fortunate swing of his sword, lopping off the head of one and an arm off the other.

To Maeze's dismay, two of the remaining four Banelings had just now realized what he had hoped they wouldn't, the blood pooling in the shallows from Aerick's earlier injury. They began drinking, gobbling up the bloody muck greedily, copiously consuming as much muddy water as blood. Cupping it to their pale mouths hurriedly with no care for the battle around them, they did not look like deadly predators yet. Right now they resembled nothing so much as the poor souls Maeze had seen ingesting drugs in the South Quarter, in the shadows of the alley near an apothecary shop. These were drugged out, marsh demons, bent on blood. Maeze wished, not for the first time, nor the last, that this were not the life he led.

While Aerick engaged the two Banelings on the island, Maeze lurched desperately toward the two drinking Aerick's old blood floating like an oil slick on the surface of the bog. If Maeze didn't kill them soon, then he and Aerick didn't stand a chance. Once a Baneling drank enough blood, its power-fueled blood frenzy was enough to overcome many warriors, let alone a simple criminal with a mace.

With a cry of hopeless fear, Maeze reached the two drinking creatures and conveniently clubbed one to death with a massive swing of his mace, before it even knew he had arrived. The second however, raised its head and hopped backwards with a newfound speed. Maeze stared at it in dismay as he saw its milky white eyes slowly turn from pale to a bright red, the color of blood, just as its solitary white claws on the forefinger of each hand became bright red as well. The transformation was almost complete. Maeze lunged forward with a speed born from the will to survive, enough to surprise even himself, and his mace swung in a deadly, sweeping arch before crunching repulsively into the face of the almost-transformed Baneling.

He pulled his weapon free, ripping out chunks of squalid flesh as he did so, and swung again and again, beating the creature to death. He smashed it over and over until it had been thoroughly clubbed into a watery submission and sank beneath the murky waters of the fens.

Maeze turned to look at Aerick and saw him finish off his last Baneling with a stab from his sword. He stomped back through the shallows to meet his partner. The young man, his terror and horror at the afternoon's events written plainly on his face, came quickly to Maeze and gave him a hug of friendship. They were just two men, two criminals, happy to have survived what most men would not have.

"Never thought dying would hurt so much," Aerick mumbled as his shock began to wear off. They stepped into the boat and shoved off from the bank of the small island, paddling north towards the Fortress.

"It never gets any easier," Maeze murmured in return.

Aerick looked at him curiously. "You've done it too?"

"Well, near enough. Been stabbed with the Ritual Wound for bait three times if that's what you mean. Just like you were tonight. It's the only way to ensure enough of the swamp bastards come to make certain we could meet the Quota. This way, we know we killed more than enough of them for our weapons to pass the Death Tax tonight." Maeze answered, numb from the draining exhaustion of the battle as well as the fear, which sapped his strength even more.

Aerick nodded silently. He understood. He had gone through the training upon becoming a Slayer. They didn't teach you how to fight in the training. The Ruling Council didn't care much for criminals turned Slayers. But they did go out of their way to make sure you knew how to attract the slimy, sodden Banelings if you were short of the Quota for the week. The blood of a dying man attracted the swamp creatures like nothing else. They would come from miles around at the scent of blood in the water.

Maeze rowed, his mind hardly functioning, while Aerick stared just as dully at the dim, shadowy surroundings. The marsh was everything. The marsh was everywhere. As they approached the Fortress and pulled up to the Slayers' Docks on the south end of the structure, Maeze didn't even realize he had been paddling with tears streaming down his cheeks for the better part of a few hours. The tears left light colored streaks down his unshaven face, which was soiled with blood and the dirty water of the swamp crusted on it. And so Maeze cried quietly, silent tears welling up even as he secured the boat to the dock. His partner, his friend Aerick, did not say anything even though he noticed. What was a person supposed to say to the friend who had been forced to nearly kill him and then save his life as well? A Slayer—a man—earned the right to cry when he did such things as those.

Chapter Two

It was nearly nightfall by the time they secured the skiff and marched tiredly back up the docks and toward the southern gate of the Fortress. Hard-bitten soldiers watched their approach but they were not questioned upon their entry to the Fortress. Nobody was ever questioned. All living people resided in the Fortress, the soldiers were simply there to maintain an awareness against a possible Baneling assault and to, of course, police the city. The Fortress had been under martial law for longer than Maeze had been alive. Since the last massive Baneling assault, the great Surge of nearly fifty years ago, the army had taken over running the city. It made the rich feel comfortable, knowing military men protected their walls, and their streets were policed by focused troops. The destitute experienced something altogether different. To the poor man, the lowly widow, or the street urchin, martial law meant they had to watch their backs more closely than ever. Any infraction of the law earned a swift trip to a lifetime sentence in the jail cells, the only escape from that fate being to join the ranks of the Slayers.

Aerick and Maeze made their way through the southern gate and took an immediate right hand turn. They had to check in at the Reader in order to pay their Death Tax. It would not do to put off what was necessary.

"By the Forgotten Gods, I'm tired," Aerick muttered as they

entered a smaller building with an emblem of a sword and a fiery forge on the front.

"You'll probably be exhausted for most of your life, so get used to it," Maeze grumbled to his friend. Ten years older than Aerick, Maeze had gained a considerably dismal outlook on life.

Aerick waved off the statement with one careless hand as if to say he didn't wish to discuss the implications of what Maeze was saying. Maeze didn't really blame him. His legs felt heavy too. All Maeze wished to do right now was pay the tax, establish the fact that he had met Quota, and then find a hot meal and a mug of ale before he retired to his lumpy straw mattress. Then up with the dawn to do it again. Well, hopefully not a day like today. When life was good as a Slayer, you met your quotas little by little, a kill or two a day, preventing the need for an all out melee like today at the end of the week. Hunting had been scarce this week, which had precipitated today's predicament. Days like today, while not completely uncommon, were not exactly usual. However, the fear was the same constant companion. It was always there.

The small room they entered was dim and smoky. It looked like a normal smithy. Forge on one end with a bellows ready to pump, there were tools and implements of a smith hanging on the walls, as well as an anvil placed conveniently near the forge, with a quenching barrel nearby. It was a smithy, the smithy of the Slayers, but it served a double function.

"Slayers Maeze and Aerick here to pay the weekly tax, Sir." Maeze, the senior of the partnership, addressed the very heavily muscled smith who was cleaning his shop as he prepared to retire for the night.

The smith grunted. "Huh, cutting it close to Quota Hour, aren't you?" The man's remark about their late arrival, it was nearly dusk on the last day of the week, sparked the familiar feeling of anger coupled with hopelessness that Maeze often felt when he considered his plight. The smith peered at them suspiciously. Late arrivals sometimes didn't actually have enough Death Tax in their Slayer weapons to meet the Quota and a military presence was needed. As if in response to that very idea, the smith reached up to a bell on the wall, grasped the rope string attached to the knocker and clanged it back and forth twice, the metal note reverberating in the night air. In a heartbeat, ten soldiers filed in from a small barracks to the back of the building. They piled into the smithy through a small back door and took up positions at every corner of the room. Some carried axes, many swords. A few even held their short bows at the ready as if Maeze and Aerick were the most dangerous men in the Fortress. Well, Maeze supposed, it was not unheard of for Slayers to lose their mental capacity. More than one disgruntled Slayer had lashed out violently when not able to pay his tax come week's end. The soldiers were to protect against violence, and to mete out justice should Maeze and Aerick not be able to meet the Quota.

"The week was slow, as was today," Maeze answered, maintaining a respectful tone, as much as he wished to voice his anger and bitterness. "In the end, we were forced to rely on the Ritual Wound and the strength of the Binding in order to attract enough Banelings to be able to meet our weekly Quota." Ritual Wounding was the process where one Slayer inflicted a mortal wound on his partner as a last, desperate measure to attract a swarm of Banelings to give the partnership a chance to kill enough of the beasts to pay the weekly Death Tax. Maeze kept his face straight and courteous as he looked at the smith.

The man's eyes widened with respect. He understood what the Ritual Wound was. It was almost legend within the walls of the

Fortress, the ability for one Slayer to inflict certain death upon their partner and yet bring them back from the brink of the grave with their own ability to slay Banelings. People told stories about it over a mug of ale or a flask of brandy. They didn't know the truth of it, the horrific nature of the experience. Anger flared in Maeze's chest as always.

The smith, as if disliking his own unintended show of respect to the two Slayers in front of him, the two ex-criminals, sneered in disdain and backhanded Maeze across the face casually.

"When I want you to elaborate I will tell you. Now go, stick your weapons in the forge, and let the Reader say whether or not you two are in trouble." The smith leered nastily at them. His soldiers would be there to quickly corral the two Slayers if it should come to pass that their weapons didn't register the sufficient Death Tax.

Maeze and Aerick clumped tiredly forward on soggy boots, leaving wet marks on the already dirty, sooty floor as they approached the forge in the corner of the room. The Reader. The Reader was a forge like any other. It could be used for the crafting of simple tools and household necessities. It could shape weapons for the soldiers to hold on the walls of the Fortress as they protected the people from a Baneling assault. Yet this forge was also different. It was ancient for one thing. Scratches and pockmarks bit into its body, and the wear and tear of what appeared to be centuries of use made its age clear. It was the recipient of Maeze's love and hate. Yes, the Binding was dirty magic, filthy magic that enforced a form of slavery and servitude, yet that very Binding was what had enabled he and his partner to survive the day's insanity, to survive their brush with hell. It was a circular argument. On the one hand, the Reader was what had given the Ruling Council the idea and ability to create the caste of soldiers known as the Slayers, so in a sense, all of Maeze's anger could be traced back to this object as a source of all that was wrong. Yet on the other hand, Maeze supposed that eventually the Ruling Council might have reached the same conclusion of forcing criminals outside the city walls to do the dirty work of society. Maeze shuddered to think what life as a Slayer might be like without the last comfort of knowing the Binding had taken place between partners and that their lives as they fought Banelings were just a hint safer than they would be without that magic. His mixed emotions battled within him as he stood in front of the aged source of magic. The only magic left in the world.

Just as Maeze and Aerick were about to thrust their weapons back into the Reader, the forge from which they were specially, mystically, created, a man strode in through the front door of the smithy.

He was dressed in a crisp, clean, velvet shirt that was black to match his tight fitting black breeches. He wore a sword at one hip and a stout, handy cudgel on the other. Completely bald, yet with a full and well groomed golden beard on his face, he was often mistaken for being portly. But any who deemed the Grand Investigator fat were making a serious error. A soldier who had risen through the ranks to a place of prominence, he was stout. A firm belly that was large but not fat. He was a fighting man who had simply been fed well, lending him extra weight with which to use should a conflict occur, yet not taking anything away from his speed and strength. Maeze had seen him beat a number of petty thieves into submission on the streets without blinking an eye or breaking a sweat. Maeze swallowed hard, waiting for the commander of the armed forces of the Fortress to speak.

"Slayer Maeze," the Grand Investigator spoke Maeze's name with obvious distaste. "Rather late to be meeting Quota, is it not?"

Maeze was the longest serving Slayer of over three years, so even someone important such as the Grand Investigator had learned his name.

"Yes, Sir. Hunting was slow this week. Barely met the tax, Sir." Maeze kept his responses short and polite. He had learned the hard way not to anger the Grand Investigator.

"Well, that remains to be seen." The Grand Investigator nodded toward the Reader, voicing his remark with a rather nasty delight. "The Reader has not yet verified that you met the Quota." The Grand Investigator spoke with the language of a commoner who had worked his way to the top—Maeze couldn't begrudge him that concession—but once in a place of influence had done everything in his power to alter his mannerisms and speech to mimic the upper class. It was a classic case of attempting to hide one's caste origination.

Aerick stayed silent the entire time, a slight flicker of doubt and fear crossing his face as Maeze answered. "Right you are, Sir. But I assure you we have killed enough Banelings today for our weapons to register the sufficient Death Tax." Courteous. Maeze would be courteous even if he had to swallow the bile rising in his throat at being forced to talk with this monster. The Grand Investigator commanded the army and therefore the force that policed the Fortress. The primary function of the law enforcement was to find anyone breaking infraction that could be corralled and thrown into prison and then coerced into joining the Slayers. The Grand Investigator had practically built the Slayers from the ground up, not actually originating it, but still fleshing the unit out and bolstering its ranks significantly.

"Indeed." The Grand Investigator clenched his jaw as if even Maeze's polite response carried some hidden cause for anger.

"Well," he motioned impatiently, "go on, prove your merit for the week."

With a nod, Maeze and Aerick quickly shoved their weapons into the forge. Together the sword and mace entered the Reader. Maeze jerked his head at his friend and partner, and Aerick stepped quickly to the bellows and pumped a few times, then once more for good measure. The forge was silent for a moment, and the Grand Investigator and the smith along with the soldiers surrounding them, smiled cruelly, believing Maeze to have lied in saying he and Aerick had met the Quota. Maeze could see the soldiers changing their grips on their weapons and standing ready for conflict.

But then the air forced into the forge by the bellows swirled slightly around their weapons, caressing them, and creating a sound. It was a strange sound, as if heard from a long way off. First there was a gurgling bark and a keening wail, then the sound of a human scream. Maeze could recognize that it was his own shrill voice making the noise. Next, there was a crunch and splat, the wet sounds of a marshland battle. The sounds of the battle from a few hours earlier, replayed themselves in dreadful accuracy, every grunt, shuffle of feet, every scream and wail, it could all be heard as if watched from a great distance. The faces of the soldiers and the two officials grew sour as they realized indeed, Maeze and Aerick had put up a tremendous fight and had likely met the Quota. The sickening sounds of the battle trailed off as the resonance of the fight, contained within the weapons wore out. The bellows had forced the air into the forge, the Reader, and set the reading into motion. The sounds had been Read, all that was left now was to see the outcome, to see if the weapons registered the sufficient Death Tax. If Maeze had miscounted—though he was almost certain he had not— they would be punished, probably killed. The light of the fire in the forge would glow reddish, the color of blood, should punishment of any kind be the verdict. However, if they met the tax, if the magic in their weapons registered the required amount of Baneling dead, the coals and fire of the forge would swirl a mix of white and blue flames.

Maeze held his breath until as if stirred by a great wind, the flames of the Reader billowed upwards, flashing white with a flicker of cobalt in the coals as well. Sparks scattered from the mouth of the reader to punctuate the fact that the two Slayers had passed. They had killed enough Banelings this week in order to pass the reading.

"It appears this time you have paid the toll, Slayer," the smith muttered angrily. "The Reader never lies. Its flames can read the number of dead Banelings in the metal of your weapons as easily as you could read a book. Well," he grinned viciously, "maybe not like you. You probably can't read a lick."

"Well, what are the odds of that?" the Grand Investigator smirked, seeming to have recovered from his frustration from before. "It appears even a hopeless Slayer such as you, Maeze, has survived to, shall I say, slay another day," the official quipped, his full yet well groomed beard moved as he laughed. The soldiers around the room laughed like sycophants at his jest.

Maeze just stared at the man who controlled his life as a Slayer with as much dignity and tranquility as possible. He wanted to avoid any angry outbursts that might lead to punishment. All he wanted was a full belly and a bed right now.

Surprisingly, it was the young Aerick who spoke up. Almost as if his words came to his lips unbidden, the youthful Slayer asked, "Why do you treat him...us, so?"

Maeze closed his eyes in chagrin. Why couldn't the lad have kept his mouth shut? Wasn't being alive this evening, after all they had been through, enough of a blessing? Did he have to tempt fate further?

The Grand Investigator swiveled his head immediately, his attention jumping from Maeze to Aerick. He answered with a silken hiss, like a snake approaching its prey, "Because, soldier, people like you need to be put in your place. We," the Grand Investigator motioned to the soldiers and smith around them, "are your betters. As such, you should show us due respect and homage." He sneered at the young Slayer.

"But," began Aerick, and Maeze groaned inwardly at the youth's inability to let it rest and leave well enough alone, "we risk our lives for you every day." Now Aerick was beginning to grow angry. Maeze could see that today's events had shaken his partner's understanding of the world and society, of his place as a Slayer. Nearly dying just to lure the inhabitants of a swampy netherworld as they lusted after your blood, could do that to a man. Maeze remembered the first time he had received the Ritual Wound. It had been the turning point when he realized he had not actually escaped the cell, he just inhabited an unseen prison now, one with more inhabitants, the likes of which were horrifying beyond imagining. He could tell Aerick was just now realizing the price he had paid by becoming a Slayer.

"Yes. You do what I say, when I say. If I want you to fight an army of Banelings all by yourself with nothing but your hands, you'll do that too Slayer. Are we clear?" The Grand Investigator didn't wait to see if he got the response he wanted from Aerick, simply assuming what he wanted would come to pass. Aerick's anger smoldered, Maeze could tell by the look on his partner's face, as the official turned his attention back to Maeze. He prayed his friend would be quiet.

"And you, Slayer Maeze, you should attempt to model better behavior for your young partner." The Grand Investigator lashed out with a closed fist and bloodied Maeze's face, sending him reeling into the waiting arms of one of the soldiers behind him. The soldier caught him and laughed evilly, then threw him back to his feet toward the Grand Investigator.

The official continued, "Good dog. There's the kind of subservience I want from a grunt." Maeze fought the urge to fight back. It would do no good. Forgetting his pride he stayed silent. The Grand Investigator chuckled darkly. "We've trained you well." He backhanded Maeze again casually as if just to prove his point then spoke further. "Criminals like you deserve a second chance." He smiled in mock innocence and benevolence, "and we, the merciful Ruling Council, give it to you in the form of your job as a Slayer." He smiled. "Now, isn't that generous of us?"

"Very, Sir." Maeze forced his voice to be smooth.

"Oh, you're good, Slayer, you hide your anger well. But remember, I caught you once when you were thieving on the streets, and I can sniff out your disloyal thoughts easier than you care to imagine." Done speaking, he made a show of dusting off Maeze's tunic and straightening it as if he was a caring, older brother, and then he reached his open palm up to lightly slap Maeze's cheek lightly to emphasize his last point.

"Are we clear, Slayer?"

"Indeed we are, Sir."

The Grand Investigator left with the smith who ran the Slayer's forge on some matter of business, taking the troop of soldiers with him as well as an honor guard. Just like that, Maeze and his partner were left alone in the room to collect their weapons, glowing with a pale iridescent light in the aftermath of their Reading, and exit the building.

As soon as they left the smithy, scents assailed their nostrils. Maeze tilted his head back and inhaled luxuriously. Aerick did the same. All day, every day spent out on the marsh with only the fetid reek of the fens and bogs around to fill one's nose made a person thankful for good smells when they breathed them in. Well, better smells he amended in his mind. Not all smells in the Fortress were pleasant, but nearly all were better than the scent of brown water, muck, and murky vegetation, rotting together into one infernal landscape. Here, the smells of the evening ran rampant on the breeze. The Fortress, standing upon its island, was divided into four sections: the north quarter, south quarter, and east and west quarters. The north side of the Fortress was the only wall made of stone and was slightly higher. Therefore, it was looked upon as being safer, more secure. The north quarter had evolved into an upper class neighborhood. If he and Aerick even showed their faces there, especially after dark, the night patrols would toss them back into whichever quarter from which they had come. The upper class didn't like riffraff in their section of the city.

The east and south quarters were filled with the middle class and soldiers, families who were just making ends meet. The west quarter was where Maeze and his partner now headed. The poor district. It was the den of street thugs and petty criminals. The Grand Investigator delighted in sending his patrols through there often to try and scramble up a few new prisoners to recruit into the Slayers' unit. Recruit was a lenient word for what they did. Maeze had heard many rumors lately of even honest folk being arrested, framed on trumped up charges just so the Grand Investigator could bolster the ranks of his Slayer unit and put the upper class citizens' minds at ease. The rationale of the high society was, the more Slayers there were, then the less likely there would be a Baneling assault, since the whole idea behind the Slayer unit was to thin the population of the Banelings by constant hunting. They didn't care who they sent out to do their dirty work. Bakers turned bookies, were caught and imprisoned then drafted into the Slayers. They were used just as soon as ex-soldiers gone rogue, even prostitutes who might have offended the wrong upper class client, were forced into the Slaying business. It was sickening. And there was nothing Maeze could do about it.

"Didn't that make you angry?" Aerick was asking as they strode wearily into the west quarter. "I hate the Grand Investigator." He was an impulsive youth.

"What use is there to getting angry? Anger just gets me dead quicker than my job as a Slayer will," Maeze responded with his usual attempt to temper his partner's rash emotions.

"But don't you want to do something about it all?"

"What is there to do?" Maeze waited for an answer from his friend but got none. Aerick just rubbed his hand over his short, coarse, black hair and seemed lost in thought, slightly daunted by the question. Aerick was a great one for 'somedays' and 'somethings,' but when it came time to think practically and execute a plan he often fell short. He clearly was frustrated by the official's treatment of them, but it was just the way it was. He didn't realize yet that there was no changing the system. The poor stayed poor, the destitute were exploited, and the Ruling Council sat in their soft sedan chairs and got fat off the sweat and sacrifice of others.

They entered the west quarter. Home. One could smell the street odors wafting by on the night breeze. Narrow streets and high, crooked buildings clogged the skyline. The Fortress was all there was. There was no room to expand, so the streets were crowded by over hanging buildings. Long ago the Ruling Council had realized this Fortress, this island, was all there was in the world. The surrounding area was all marsh and fen, bogs that would suck a man under, with tiny islands floating about, too small for the construction of anything worthwhile. Not to mention the Banelings. Survival depended upon defending the Fortress.

The smell of poor sanitation, stinking sewers, and gutters rank with filth, mixed with the scent of street vendors selling their wares. Fried taro root emitted a hearty aroma, fish stews, boiled in cauldrons and pots in dark alleyways seasoned the air with scents of their spices: arrowleaf, mint, sea grape, and cranberry. There was also dandelion seasoned dark meat, which was probably dog or maybe rat, while boiled cattails and rushes were sold in bunches to those who could afford nothing else. Rice and beans and oats aplenty formed the platform for many of those foods.

It was dirty and smelly, but it was home. Maeze had grown up on these streets. His first attempt at thieving had been in an alley not far from where they walked now. He had pickpocketed in the taverns to survive after he realized circumstances, and life in general really, weren't going his way. Then the Grand Investigator and his men had captured him. There were no second chances, whatever the Grand Investigator liked to say. It was life in prison for Maeze or a life fighting hellish creatures of the nether realm day after day. That wasn't much of a choice or a chance, he thought grimly, bitterly.

The silence seemed to have stretched long enough for Aerick because he spoke breaking the quiet. "Hungry? Want to sit down and get a bite somewhere?"

Maeze made a face to show he wasn't sure. "We might as well

just grab something cheap on the way home. Tomorrow, it's another day of Slaying and we'll need our rest." Maeze spoke as he eyed the boiled cattails he passed. His pay, one copper a day was hardly enough to afford anything. Maybe he could splurge and get some fish soup. He thought about it, but then decided against it. Rushes and cattails it was tonight.

"You're right of course," Aerick agreed quickly. "But what about a drink then. Mug of ale? I'm buying."

"Don't be stupid, Aerick," Maeze said, perhaps a bit too harshly, "you can't afford to pay for yourself, let alone me, any more than I can. Instead, save your money and buy something nice for the girl you've been making eyes at down near the docks."

Aerick smiled, somewhat wistfully. "Myra is pretty, isn't she? You're full of good ideas." He clapped Maeze on the shoulder. "Maybe I will buy her something."

Maeze noted with relief that his partner had returned to his usual good humor after their miserable day. He was young. He could still bounce back from an ordeal like today and think tomorrow would be better, that the future might hold something different. Maeze was old enough, experienced enough, to realize the truth. Life didn't get better. It didn't often change, except for the worse. Even horrific days like today would be forgotten, like the old gods in the meaningless dearth of days they would possess as Slayers.

They bypassed the taverns, alight with torches and filled with the raucous shouts of drunken men and only slightly more sober bar wenches. The taverns were a wild place, their occupants the perfect fodder for the Grand Investigator's pledge to the Ruling Council that he would build the Slayers until the threat of

Banelings was gone altogether.

Finally, Maeze reached his alley and grunted goodnight to his partner as they parted ways, Aerick walking a few blocks farther to reach his own room. Maeze ducked into the alley and then opened the door to his home. It was a below ground entry to a cellar room. Once it had held food stores, but as food had dwindled in recent years it had been converted to a room for rent. A single room, with no windows, earth walls and a lone hay mat in the corner. It was bleak. Yet, it was home. The only other garnish in the room was the chamber pot in the corner, but as often as not, Maeze just used the street a few steps above. It was dirty and musty, it was dank and dark and full of bugs, but at least it was a place of peace and quiet.

Maeze kicked off his boots and flopped onto the hard mat stuffed with hay. It was lumpy and firm, but after a day like today it felt softer and lusher than anything he had ever felt before in his entire life. He closed his eyes and drifted off with the sounds of a street fight in the alley above his head, the racket not loud enough to drown out the beckoning calls of sleep.

Chapter Three

The tolling of the bell woke Maeze sometime in the middle of the night. The alarm bell. The call to arms. Maeze was a Slayer, and that meant he was also in the army. All Slayers were soldiers too. When the call to arms came, he was required to answer just like every other honest soldier within the Fortress wall.

Maeze grabbed his boots and pulled them onto his feet. They were still damp from the fight in the marsh yesterday, but he was accustomed to it. Life as a Slayer was spent on the opaque water of the fens, and one grew accustomed to not being dry. He couldn't remember the last time he had been completely dry.

He rushed up the few stairs to the alleyway above his cellar room, clutching his mace tightly in his hands. A call to arms could mean only one thing: a Baneling assault. The assaults happened every couple of months. It was the reason the Slayers existed; to thin the population of the Banelings on a daily basis so that when the time came for the Fortress to repel an assault—and the time always came eventually because Banelings were mindless in their quest for human blood—the Fortress would be able to stand and hold firm.

The streets of the city were abundant with activity even though it was the middle of the night. Street children ran about between the legs of people as they played together their games in the dark. Their mothers were likely whores who couldn't mind them at night so they had free run of the quarter. The west quarter was always alive even at night. People were still selling the same cart food on the sides of the narrow streets, ignoring the rain that threatened to pour down from the thick clouds above obscuring the night sky. Vendors sold wares, taverns burst at the seams with drinkers, carousing until the dawn light broke. Not all the quarters were such, the south could get unruly like the west, but the east and especially the north quarters were much more decorous.

Maeze rushed through the streets along with a large number of other previously off duty soldiers, in his stained tunic and ragged breeches, rumpled from a few hours of sleep without removing them. The bell tolled again, three sharp notes, the general call to arms, followed by one long drawn out bell toll indicating the north wall was the location in need of defense. Maeze rushed along with the other soldiers and Slayers who resided in the west quarter as they hurried to reach the north wall where their strength of arms was needed.

Before long, Aerick fell in beside Maeze. "Morning already, you mangy bastard," he said and nudged Maeze with his shoulder in camaraderie, his usual bright self, yesterday's events seemingly forgotten, at least for now.

Maeze grunted in assent. Indeed it was morning for them now. A few hours sleep was all they would get. "Do you have to always be so damn cheerful?" he asked his partner.

Aerick grinned. "What use is there to being angry? Life is too short to be bitter all the time."

"You seemed fairly distraught and frustrated last night."

Aerick frowned, then brightened. "Well, that was then and this is now."

Maeze shook his head and laughed sardonically. "As long as you're happy, I guess that works for you."

They ran on together in silence, leaving the west quarter and entering the north district. Muddy, soggy alleys, unpaved and littered with debris gave way to well kept cobblestoned streets. The quality of the roads wasn't the only difference between the west quarter and the north quarter—the poor district and the rich. The north quarter was also groomed, cleaned, the buildings not stained with the dirty soot of street vendors cooking their foods to sell. The rich section of the city was all tight and compact like the rest of the city, but it was done so in an elegant way. Spotless, architecturally beautiful apartments overhung jewelry shops and grocer markets. Mansions abutted buildings of commerce and trade; there was even a cathedral.

"By the Forgotten Gods, I had forgotten how clean this place was!" Aerick exclaimed into the dark of the early morning. "Just smell the air. It's… it's fresh."

He was right. The western section of the Fortress stank of fish guts and slime, discarded into the gutters and sewers from the vendors on the streets. Feces and vomit lined the alleys and tankards of ale were carried outside of the taverns as the people spectated a bar fight and then subsequently spilled in drunkenness. The entire quarter had the stale, dank reek of alcohol permeating the refuse.

The Grand Investigator never had the place cleaned or taken care of because the environment bred criminals—it turned out desperate people like nothing else could. Those desperate, destitute criminals were eventually caught adding to the ranks of the Slayers the Grand Investigator created and commanded. The officials did everything they could to add to the chaos of the poor district. The more people that were there, then eventually the more soldiers and likely criminals-turned-Slayers they would breed. And the overriding goal was to provide a higher measure of security for the rich.

The Ruling Council had even promoted the birthing of children by offering a gold coin to each mother upon the birth of her child— bastard child or no—although the west quarter was already bulging at the seams to hold in its stinking, filthy population of degenerates. The other quarters were policed and the population restricted, leaving the north quarter, through which Maeze and his partner traveled now, spacious and under populated in comparison with poorer sections of the Fortress.

The north wall reared its ancient stone head in front of them. They reached the stairwell at the foot of the wall and began climbing along with other incoming soldiers all the while listening to the bellowing of a sergeant who was giving them their orders. The wall was grey stone, stained a dull ash and black color over the ages from all the storms and assaults it had withstood.

They reached the top of the wall and looked out as they took their ranks. There were archers manning the turrets in the tower at the center of the wall, and there were also more archers interspersed along the ramparts itself. Foot soldiers were handed spears to use in defense and Maeze hung his flanged mace from the clasp at his hip. He took his spear and surveyed the scene, planting himself firmly next to Aerick on the walls.

The marshland was barely visible in the dim light of early morning. A grey haze was only just beginning to appear on the far northern horizon and it did little to illuminate the world around them. No matter, Maeze had stood on this wall before, he knew what he would see if it were light out. The marsh would stretch forever, swamp oaks, and the occasional red gum tree, the only punctuations to the interminable amount of tiny piles of floating vegetation, reeds and rushes, and the ever-varying bog swirls and currents which played through the landscape. The marsh was all. Nothing else existed.

Maeze could see now why the alarm bell had been rung. Indeed it was an assault. Banelings were beginning to boil up from the muddy, brown water like bubbles rising to the surface of a pot of hot water. Many hundreds of them splashed and scrambled through the muck at the shallows of the island, about twenty yards from the wall. They shambled up to the wall and hammered on it dully with their pale white fists. It was a testament to their inability to think, really, that they had chosen to attack the northern wall, the only wall made of stone. The north ramparts were the highest and the most secure.

Wave upon wave of arrows from the walls and towers slaughtered the creatures from the swampy abyss and they died in droves. Their grubby white faces emitted the keening wails and the gurgling barks as if their mouths were still filled with the muddy water from whence they came. They died, and yet more came. The new arrivals climbed and shambled onwards and upwards. The dead bodies of the Banelings created a ramp of sorts that allowed the live ones to reach ever higher and higher toward the top of the wall.

As he always did, Maeze felt icy fear clamp its deathly grip around his belly as he gazed on the sight before him. Yet, the terror was nothing like what he felt when out on duty in the swamp with just his partner and a skiff. Facing even a horde of Banelings from behind the safety of a wall with an army at your back was easier than fighting them all alone with your partner prone and dying in the muck of an island far from home. It was strange to realize that despite his anxiety, he was likely still one of the calmest men on this wall. He had faced the hell before them daily, and in much more dire situations, and had prevailed. This he could do. Maeze gripped his spear confidently and prepared for the endless thrusting he knew would be required when the Banelings reached the top of the wall.

Sure enough, the battle raged higher and higher, as the creatures crawled on their mound of dead and came close enough to stab. Maeze jabbed his spear downwards, gouging out a completely white eye with his first thrust. Then again and again, and the beast beneath released a horrible wailing bark, then fell backwards to become part of the ramp for those following it.

They fought until the sun began to climb, painting brilliance across the morning sky and banishing the dark clouds of the night. The light illuminated their foes in a completely different manner, and Maeze could see the looks of fright and repulsion on the faces of some of the younger, newer soldiers to the army; fresh recruits who were facing their first minor assault. And this assault was minor, Maeze realized. Hundreds of the Banelings might sound daunting, but the wall would inevitably hold, especially since it was the north wall, the sturdy stone of days gone by. Yet this fresh assault, as each assault did every few months, reminded the Ruling Council of one thing: eventually another Surge would come, an attack of much greater proportions than any battle such as the one raging now.

The last Surge had been nearly fifty years ago, long before Maeze was ever born, but it had nearly crippled the Fortress. On that day, the fighting had spilled into the streets of all quarters.

Men and women who were not soldiers had fought for their lives with pots and pans, and rakes and butcher knives. The carnage had been vast as a swarm of thousands upon thousands of Banelings overran the walls and pillaged through the city. Eventually, the people had fought them off, killing each and every Baneling, but the cost had been great. Too great for the Ruling Council to accept—nearly a third of the human population dead—and thus the Slayers had been born when the Reader had been discovered and studied in some long forgotten basement.

"Don't they ever stop coming?" Aerick asked in exhaustion after they had been fighting for hours.

"I doubt they think enough to do anything but move forward and drink. Blood is all they know." Maeze exhaled his response as he stabbed another.

He looked hard at the Baneling climbing towards him over the heaps and piles of its brethren. It was a sickening creature, all white except for the streaks of dirty water still rolling off its body from the marsh. Its eyes were completely white as well in sunken eye sockets, its hollow cheeks with folds of fleshy skin, grubby fat belying the thinness of their frames. The Baneling drew closer and it reached one hand out and up towards the top of the wall, its single thin claw reaching, reaching for a vein to open from which to gobble and slurp up blood. Maeze cast his spear aside in disgust and unhooked his mace. He wanted to bash these creatures of the underworld with all his might. They looked like the embodiment of death reincarnate, like the shell or the husk of what a man might become were he to sink into the fetid swamp around them and marinate at the bottom for many years. Maeze smashed the clawed finger reaching towards him and then bashed the head in also as the Baneling gurgled in death, milky white liquid oozing from its wounds like blood.

48

"What are these things?" a soldier half whispered, half wailed to himself in fright beside Maeze. Maeze clubbed another of the bastards to death.

"Perhaps they're the afterlife, Soldier," Maeze answered the young man with the spear, a sarcastic smirk playing on his face. "Ever wonder what happens when you die? What happens to people when their bodies are returned to the swamp?"

The boyish soldier stared at Maeze in horror, completely swallowing the joke whole. Maeze had no idea what they were, but he keenly felt the need for a laugh of any kind, even a bitter, mocking one, at a time like this.

"It can't be, can it?" The soldier gasped. "I mean I always wondered what happened to the bodies they take out and sink in the swamp. I know they can't bury them for lack of space of the island or burn them for lack of fuel but if this is the result..." he trailed off as he stabbed another Baneling with his spear.

Suddenly, Maeze no longer felt any humor at the jest he had made to the young man. His sardonic laughter cut off as a terrible question formed in his mind. Could it really be that simple? Were the Banelings nothing more than the bodies of the dead, mutated by some sinister influence of the fens? Could something, nature, really do that?

His dark musings were cut off as a fresh wave of Banelings clambered awkwardly over their fallen brothers. A few managed to get close enough to pull some soldiers over the ramparts with their cold, slimy fingers. In revulsion, Maeze watched as a Baneling plunged one of its lone, slender claws into the neck of a soldier and then cupped its pale white hands underneath the flow of blood. The Baneling smeared the blood on its face as it tried to drink from the blood pooling in its hands. It was awkward, like a drunken man trying without success to put a straw in his mouth. Finally, the Baneling resulted to sticking out its sickly, white tongue and lapping at the neck of the fallen soldier like a dog. Then the beast was overwhelmed by a pack of fresh Banelings and a fight over the blood ensued.

Another and another soldier was pulled over the ramparts and fed on below. It was not enough to fear losing the wall, but it was grotesque to watch. Then the inevitable happened. One of the Banelings, as of yet still not riddled with arrows, drank enough blood from his cupped hands at the base of a man's throat, that it burst into a blood frenzy, red liquid smeared all over its face. It was not uncommon, but it was prevented at all costs. Killing Banelings before they fed on enough blood to go into a frenzy was imperative, because once they had ingested enough of the warm, red flow, they transformed. Perhaps not in form, for they looked decidedly similar to the usual Baneling appearance, the only differences were how the eyes changed completely red instead of a milky white. Also, the single claw on the tip of each forefinger—the only fingers free from webbing—transformed from translucent to a bright red the same as their eyes. Other than that they looked the same. Yet the transformation was more in power and ability than in shape or appearance. The last of the Banelings drinking blood were being felled by arrows from the archers on the wall, as well as a particularly brave contingent of soldiers who had scaled down the wall upon the bodies of the dead creatures to reach the feeding glut below. The soldiers fell upon the Banelings mercilessly, chopping off heads and hands, cleaving bodies until the creatures were killed before being able to make the change into a blood frenzy. All but three that is.

Three of the Banelings, having swallowed enough of the blood of the fallen humans to make the transformation complete, looked up with their brilliantly red eyes, eyes which suddenly lost the deadness which they normally possessed, to be replaced by a look of insatiable hunger. They flexed their hands and fingers as they watched the arrows and the soldiers methodically dismember, disembowel, and in general, altogether dispose of their brethren, before making their move.

Maeze had only seen a Baneling in full blood frenzy a few times. When a Slayer saw such an event outside the walls while on duty, it usually meant his death. Slayers didn't survive long when the Banelings attained blood lust. He had only seen it briefly during a few stints along the walls during previous assaults.

He watched with apprehension as the three Banelings, once mindless, wandering freaks of nature, suddenly became rational, powerful creatures of the nether world. It was as if the blood cleared their minds and reasoned with their thoughts until they could think and function like a sentient being—all except for the insatiable thirst for more blood. Nothing could override their primal urge to feed.

"By the Forgotten Gods," Aerick breathed in stunned fright as he witnessed his first blood frenzy.

The group of brave soldiers, who had disposed of the Banelings drinking the blood, seemed to realize they had arrived just a moment too late to finish off all of the creatures before the transformation took place. For an instant, the soldiers and the trio of transformed Banelings stared at each other across the few feet of space separating them, and then like fog clearing as the sun broke through on a cloudy day their thoughts seemed to clear. The human soldiers screamed in fear as they saw their doom awaiting them. The men turned to rush and scramble back up the pile of dead Baneling bodies leading back to the ramparts, a few even dropping their weapons in their haste to reach the apparent safety of the Fortress walls.

A chill passed through Maeze's heart as he noticed with distinct discomfort an evil smile creep across the pale, white face of one of the transformed Banelings. The three Banelings absolutely possessed by the blood lust now, ignored the arrows that had begun raining down upon them, brushing them aside as if gnats with a hand. Some of the arrows found their mark and stuck, and when they did, this time, fresh, red blood poured out of the Banelings bodies instead of the milky white ooze Maeze normally saw. The Banelings broke off many of the tips of the arrows and continued forward falling upon the fleeing soldiers with a reckless abandon, fueled by the desire for more blood. They resembled pincushions, but the blood they had ingested strengthened them, enabling them to withstand much more than the usual amount of punishment their bodies could endure. They moved with speed and swiftness, their steps sure and lithe now, with none of the former clumsy, ungainly movements. Physical ineptitude left behind, the Banelings in blood frenzy slashed the veins of the fleeing men, and drank their blood with precision and accuracy of their mouths. No blood was wasted this time as they continued to ignore the arrows lodging in their flesh now empowered by human blood.

White and sickly, their graceful movements belied their appearance. With a gigantic leap, the three Banelings left behind all their fallen comrades. They cleared the wall in one effortless bound and landed on the cobblestoned streets of the north quarter, all awkwardness left in the marsh behind them. They would stay like that until they were killed or they'd drunk their fill and returned to their swampy dens, to resume their normal forms. As they landed, they turned away from the wall and soldiers, almost as if innately understanding that the easy meat, the fresh blood, lay before them in the city ahead, rather than in the sharp steel and grim faces of the fearful soldiers manning the wall.

"Follow them, quickly!" A desperate sergeant cried out, ordering his frozen troops. The man, no doubt, realized that his job, and even his very life, might be determined by what happened next. The Ruling Council was not particularly gentle with people, officers or common, who they deemed to have failed them.

But the rush of soldiers heading bleakly for the stairs to reach the streets upon which the Banelings now stood could not move quickly enough. Once again, Maeze witnessed with chilling effect, a Baneling with blood red eyes and a scarlet claw on each hand, smile a nasty grin to its fellow blood-frenzied brethren and then dash down a side street with incredible speed. The other two Banelings stayed only long enough to kill a few soldiers and lick the blood from their fingers before leaving. They spun with extreme agility and grace, speed and precision, their claws rending tears in necks and wrists, joints and muscles, as they ripped through a squadron of troops with an ease that was directly in opposition of their normal shambling, slow gait. Then as if mischief and mayhem awaited them, they each flashed off in a ball of white in different directions, about to cause an uproar in the defenseless city beyond.

With the Banelings gone, off to rampage through an unsuspecting city, Maeze collapsed against the ramparts, gazing at the carnage beyond. Hundreds of dead denizens of the swamp lay in heaps and piles, a virtual ramp leading to the top of the city wall. The men had defended well and had not lost many soldiers since the creatures normally attacked with the mindless oblivion of the living dead. Only the three surviving Banelings in blood frenzy would cause trouble, yet Maeze had a hunch that the havoc they would wreak in the unsuspecting city would have longer lasting and farther-reaching effects than anyone thought. He didn't know why, but his instincts told him something bad was brewing.

The sergeants were still yelling and men were piling down the stairs to begin the hunt for the three hellish creatures, but at the moment Maeze and his partner were nowhere near an exit and had a moment to rest while they waited their turn to descend.

"I thought it was only myth, the blood frenzy." Aerick gasped through chilled, chattering teeth. A frozen, morning wind had picked up from the north and it carried the stench of dead Banelings up over the ramparts and into the faces of the men holding the wall.

"It's no legend, lad. Though I wish it were," Maeze sighed sadly. "This bodes ill for us, the low born. I can feel it in my bones."

"How do you mean?"

Maeze directed a piercing look at his friend. "What quarter is this?" He indicated the cobbled streets and well kept buildings in front of them.

"The north, of course." Aerick looked at him questioningly.

Maeze waited to see if he would follow the train of thought on his own. The young Slayer's blank look showed he would not. Maeze took him a step further in thought. "Who lives in the north quarter?"

"The rich. I'm not stupid, Maeze. You're going somewhere with this so just spit it out."

"Very well," Maeze said. "The first targets of those Banelings are bound to be upper class. The city will be in an uproar after this." He paused to look at the city within the walls of the Fortress. "It's only three Banelings, but they are in the blood frenzy. It's not the same, not as bad as a Surge, no doubt," he indicated the dead creatures beyond the wall. "It's not like a host of the beasts are loose within the city walls, no, we held firm. But those three Banelings will definitely do damage. Many people will die before they're quelled, and I'd be willing to bet that a significant portion of those dead will be rich."

"So?" Aerick asked. The young man still didn't see. He was naïve.

"All I know, Partner, is when the rich die, the poor pay. Something bad is going to come of this, just wait and see."

Aerick's face took on an aspect of apprehension, then worry as he gazed at the city. Screams shook the early morning air. The sounds pierced the air from afar, the noises of men and women startled by the ferocity of their deaths, unsuspecting citizens unaware that hell's inhabitants were loose in the city. Maeze closed his eyes in dismay. The rich would die. Those Banelings in the north quarter would kill without discrimination. They held no regard for any class of man. But the poor would pay, Maeze was somehow surer of that than he could explain. It was true, a fact fixed in his mind. One he could not shake loose. The Ruling Council always found a way to make life worse for the bottom feeders of their city.

"You men," a sergeant commanded insultingly, his upper class accent clear and precise in contrast to the slurred, aspirated words and syllables of Maeze and many of the other soldiers' common tongue. "We are leaving one company to man the walls and clear away this rubble." He indicated the dead Banelings beyond. "You soldiers have been selected." The sergeant made as if to turn away and then glanced back again. "Oh, and make sure those bastards are dead before you lug them out and sink them in the swamp." The officer finished his orders and dismissed them to their duties.

Maeze and Aerick, along with a handful of other troops, kept a vigil eye from the wall, watching the northern horizon, making sure another threat wasn't imminent. It was unlikely to have another assault for months, but caution always paid off. Maeze watched as many of the remaining troops began clearing away the dead creatures, putting them into boats brought up from the docks and taking them out to sink them in the dark, murky waters beyond.

He watched as the cold wind blew the northern wind from the frozen marshes. He watched and listened to the sounds of fighting and death from the city quarter behind him. Eventually the Banelings would be destroyed, but they had not been disposed of yet. He stared resolutely out at the landscape with a sinking heart. Life was hard already, but he had a feeling it was about to get even worse. And when things grew worse, it usually meant the life of a Slayer became even more difficult. They were the refuse, the garbage of the city. Criminals—deserving or not of such a label— they had been drafted into the service of the Fortress and nothing would change that now.

Maeze watched the marsh, he felt the wind, heard the shouts of pain and agony from behind him as he faced the landscape ahead of him. And all the while, uncharacteristically, he dreamed of a better future. It was not like him to place his mind or faith in anything less than stable reality. Yet, as he reflected on what had just happened, he had a feeling that anything less than daydreams and wishful thinking would see Maeze's heart and mind plunge into a dreadful abyss of despair and oblivion and numbness. Such were the difficulties lying ahead. And so with a heavy heart and a frightened mind, Maeze dreamed; he dreamed about tomorrow.

Chapter Four

"I didn't do it, I swear!" The young man was almost a boy still; he could hardly have been past twelve years old. Wrists in irons, he was being dragged away between two soldiers. "Let me go, this isn't fair!" He was practically wailing now, weeping and sobbing as he went. He had reason to cry indeed.

Maeze didn't know the young man being hauled away by the Grand Investigator's troops. He didn't know if the charges of thievery were true or false. Whether the accusations were real or trumped up, the boy certainly appeared to be distraught. His fear and bitterness at an unfair arrest seemed genuine. Yet, Maeze had seen other accused criminals act the same, men Maeze had known for a fact to be guilty of the criminal activities of which they were accused. Criminals usually knew how to act. In the end it didn't really matter. Whether or not the youth had been arrested on real or fake evidence was irrelevant. Once a man was arrested by the Grand Investigator, he stayed arrested. No amount of begging, crying, or threatening could make it otherwise. Lately, there had even been arrests of women, as the Grand Investigator's men had been cracking down on the west quarter in an alarmingly harsh manner.

The soldiers disappeared with the arrested lad around a corner and Maeze continued about his business. His boots were being mended by old Lady Merryweather. Her name was not very indicative of reality—she wasn't much of a lady and she was hardly ever merry, no matter the weather. She would be displeased if he was late. Her foul mouth and coarse language were rough on poor ears. Maeze had gathered a handful of wild plants as promised, on one of his daily hunting excursions with Aerick, in order to barter for her services.

Barefoot, Maeze turned the corner, his feet pressing into the muck of the muddy streets of the west quarter, mud and slime squishing up between his toes. It would be good to get his boots back. He walked another three blocks, past broken down tenant buildings and windows, which were gaping holes in the walls. He strode by the vendors selling their boiled or fried wares. He trudged wearily by the taverns with prostitutes lining the corners, selling their pleasures for a few coppers or the promise of a hot meal. Times were hard in the west quarter. Even the south quarter, a step above the west, was in dire times. Deprivation hit everyone and people were resorting to desperate measures. Maeze had never seen it so bad. It didn't help either, that the Grand Investigator's men were everywhere as well.

Nearly a week had passed since the assault, and the Ruling Council had indeed stepped up recruitment for the Slayers unit. They didn't call it that, of course. They broadcasted their desire to 'clean the streets' and 'make the quarters a safer, more secure place for all to live'. Yet all knew exactly what their true agenda was. They were on a witch-hunt to ferret out every possible man, and even woman sometimes, available to draft into the Slayers. The Grand Investigator's troops were arresting people left and right. Sometimes on real evidence, but often as not on hearsay and second or third hand accounts of an event. It was a veritable festival of fear in the west quarter as not a man or woman went about their business without being terrified of the possibility that they might be framed for a crime they didn't commit and thrown into a jail cell to await their offer of life imprisonment or a ticket to a job as a Slayer.

Ironically, this was one of the few times Maeze felt less frightened than the average person. Daily life as a Slayer was full of fear. The fear that each day on duty might be the day the dreaded, white, clammy hands grasped him tightly and pulled him under the dark waters of the marsh. Yet, walking around with that familiar worry in his breast, Maeze realized he functioned with less anxiety than the common folk of the poor district. After all, he was already a Slayer, so what more could the Ruling Council do to him to make his life worse? But the average person lived in fear that today might be the day his life as a free man ended.

Maeze reached the room of old Lady Merryweather. He knocked on the door with a sharp rap of his knuckles. The door was half rotten and gave slightly beneath his fist. It sounded dully, without the usual pop of a firm, new door, yet the old lady heard him anyways.

"That had better be you, Maeze," Merryweather said amid a string of curses from behind the door. Maeze heard a noise, which must have been her struggling to reach the door and open it. "I've been waiting here all morning and I've better things to do than waste my time waiting for you. When a job's done, it's time to move on to the next, and I've had these boots done and fixed for too long now."

The old lady opened the door and the rest of her words were clear and easier to hear than the first, which had been spoken through the closed door. "After all, an old woman has to keep busy. I'm not young and fair enough to get by just selling my wares anymore." She cupped her sagging breasts and leered at him with a crooked grin, clearly implying what she meant by wares. Stories said she had been a whore of epic proportions when younger and had slept her way through an entire guard of soldiers. Stories also said she had even slept with the High Magistrate. Maeze didn't know if the tales were true or not. It didn't really matter to him. Despite it all, he liked Merryweather. She fixed boots well and darned clothes neatly also. Maeze didn't mind looking out for her and grabbing a handful of roots and edible vegetation or some wild grains from a floating island when he had the chance. The old lady had looked out for him when he was a kid after all, giving him a kind word or a pat on the head when he had needed it. Turn and turn about, that was what Maeze figured.

"It's me alright," Maeze said with the best grin he could muster. It was hard to smile for real these days.

"Pathetic," the old lady snorted as she watched his attempt at joviality. "You can't even fake a decent smile for an old lady."

"I do my best," Maeze answered truthfully, the forced grin fading from his face to be replaced by a look of grim resolve. "Things are tough these days. Even for those of us who had already joined the ranks of the Slayers long before the last assault."

She grunted in assent. "You're a good boy. I'm just jesting, just jesting my boy," she trailed off as old people do, repeating words she had already said. Her saggy folds of skin were drooping on her face and the grey hair on her head was wispy and sticking out all over. She turned and motioned him to follow her into the dark interior of her room.

It was a first floor room of a tenant building. It had one window, no glass, a washbasin, a small table and a bed. Maeze's boots lay on the ground by her bed, the hole in the toe patched and ready to be worn again.

"Thanks, Lady Merryweather," Maeze said politely, as he picked up his boots. He had already given her payment of the wild oats upon purchase of her services, but he laid another small bundle of wild mint, and even a few rushes he had yanked up by the roots on the table for her. They could be boiled and eaten and the mint would flavor them well.

Her eyes brightened at the sight. "Good boy, you are," she said again fondly, reaching up to pat his face. Her curses and bluster from before seeming to have faded in the sight of his extra payment. Even her pretended hurry to get on to another piece of work was gone; likely it had been an act for his benefit. Merryweather adored her reputation as a fiery old woman. She didn't like it known, but she could actually be rather sweet when the right opportunity presented itself.

"So lad, tell me about your life."

Maeze didn't really know where to begin. He stared at her blankly, a questioning look.

"Oh, come now, speak up," the old lady urged. "Have you a girl?"

Maeze shook his head. "No, Merryweather," he responded politely, "leastwise not one for longer than a night." The old lady cackled wickedly, relishing his comment, having been a woman of the night for many years in her youth. Perhaps her trade hadn't been by choice, but she hadn't exactly bucked at the obligations it had necessitated of her.

Her laughing subsided and she looked at him seriously. She pinched his arm. "Are you eating enough? Getting your rest? Are they working you too hard?" She fired the questions in quick succession, not giving him enough time to answer before the next question arrived, yet somehow managing at the same time to appear offended that he had failed to answer. It was a trick of which only old women knew the mastery.

"Yes. No. And always," he replied to the questions with a sardonic grimace. She laughed again at his honesty.

Maeze continued, following up by elaborating on his answer to the third question. "The Grand Investigator is swelling the ranks of the Slayers with new blood. Five new partnerships added this week and many more to follow if his arrest numbers are any indication."

Merryweather snorted. "Buzzard." She spat venomously. "He's arresting decent folk just minding their own business. I wouldn't be surprised to find myself in a jail cell and awaiting a trip to the Slayers unit, and me a woman and nigh on sixty years old."

Maeze could do nothing but agree with her statement. "All that is true, Merryweather. Plus he is working the Slayers harder than ever. The weekly Quota of fourteen dead Banelings per partnership has been increased to twenty and word is the Death Tax will jump yet again before the weeks out. It's getting hard and harder to make it back alive each day." He grinned weakly at the old woman's sad looking face, feeling the desire to make her laugh, but not quite managing to do so, as he joked faintly, "One of these days you'll wake to find me gone in the swamp, never to return, then you'll be free from patching up my worn boots."

The old lady cupped his cheek with a weathered hand. "Don't go getting all morbid on me now laddybuck. You've managed to survive three years as a Slayer. That's some kind of record isn't it? You'll make it years more no doubt."

He held her hand against his face, letting the motherly kindness she showed him soak in for a brief moment. Eyes closed he remembered his own mother, dead now many years and smiled at the memory. Enough. It was time to work. His boots now retrieved, it was time to go. Aerick would be waiting for him at the docks. They were still short on their number of kills this week, and the week's close was fast approaching.

He made his goodbyes to the old lady and thanked her for the boots as he put them on. Then it was off to the south quarter, to the Slayers' docks. It was a late start already and Aerick and Maeze would most likely need to stay late to have any chance of meeting Quota the next few days.

Maeze felt the familiar fear of facing the marsh chilling his spine, a sharp contradiction as he strode through the surprisingly warm, humid air. He reached the Slayers' docks and saw Aerick waiting for him near a skiff. They were the last Slayers to leave the docks, all others having already embarked on their skiffs to hunt for the day.

"Where have you been?" Aerick demanded, anxiety painting his face. "We only killed three yesterday and two the day before. None the day before that. We need the blood of fifteen more Banelings on our weapons by the day after tomorrow. If we don't hurry we'll be in real trouble." His partner's urgency was catching and Maeze hopped into the boat and let his friend push them off and begin to row.

"Sorry, I was attending to some business." He didn't really feel the need to tell Aerick about Merryweather.

His partner shrugged it off and seemed to relax a bit into his usual optimistic self. "Where to?" Aerick asked.

"West," Maeze answered shortly. "I have a good feeling about west."

Aerick shrugged and made a face as if to say west was as good as any other direction to him and pointed their course. They rowed lightly for a time, on guard as always while in the swamp, but there was no sign of Banelings around. That was always a mixed feeling for a Slayer. Banelings were terror. Fighting them was pure horror. But they were also necessary for survival. A good partnership hoped to happen across one maybe two at a time, a couple times a day. It was easier to dispose of a few Banelings at a time—not without risk to be certain—but with a greater chance of survival, both the day of and for at the end of the week also.

As if in tandem with his thoughts Maeze's young partner asked, "You ever known anybody who failed to meet Quota?"

Maeze kept staring out at their surroundings as they spoke. "Sure. Don't do this for three years and not see people come up short."

"Was it bad?"

Maeze looked bleakly at his friend's face. "What do you think?" he answered with a question.

"I think I'd rather the Banelings got me than the Grand Investigator and his thugs." Aerick shuddered as he thought.

"You sure about that?" Maeze asked quietly. "Death by torture hurts while it lasts, but even a fair bit of pain has to be better than being dragged down to the murky depths of this hellish swampland."

It was a bitter fact. The Grand Investigator used torture as punishment for those Slayers who didn't pay the Death Tax at the end of the week. If you didn't meet the Quota, you paid the tax with your own painful death. It was why most Slayers chanced the Ritual Wounding, like Maeze and Aerick had done last week, for the opportunity to attract a group of Banelings and meet the Quota. And even if it didn't work out, a sword through the belly was a better way to go, after all, than death by torture.

Aerick was quiet again for a while as they drifted westward. They passed clumps of mossy, floating vegetation. Some small islands looked firm and stable. On those, once or twice, Maeze caught sight of what looked like wild beans. That was a gold mine and they stopped to harvest a few before continuing their search for a fight.

The sun reached its midday peak, then began to sink slowly as the hours passed without a kill. They were farther out than Maeze had been in a long time, if ever, nearly a half-day's paddle from the Fortress walls.

"We'd better give thought to turning back, elsewise we'll be caught outside the walls once full dark hits. I'd not like to be deep in Baneling territory when night comes," Maeze commented to his partner.

The twilight was growing closer as Aerick nodded. "Wait a few more minutes," the young Slayer said hopefully, "then we'll turn around and go back." Maeze considered it a moment and then acquiesced.

They sat for another half of an hour, Maeze even bloodied his hand and let the red drops paint the surface of the dark water, but to no avail. Not a stir on the water or a single glimpse of a white hand or pale, fleshy skull. He sighed. Part of him was happy, a day without Banelings to fight was almost pleasant, yet the other part of him was terrified for tomorrow. What would happen when it came time to meet Quota at the end of the week?

"We better go now, Aerick," he said. "At this rate we won't reach the southern docks until a few hours after nightfall."

Aerick ignored him, staring off to the west. "What is that?" he exclaimed.

"What?" Maeze peered into the fading light, eyes searching to find whatever had so amazed his partner.

"The glow," Aerick pointed toward the horizon. "Way off in the distance."

There. Maeze saw it now. It was faint, but it was there. The sun had now sunk below the horizon, darkness encroaching, and the glow illuminated bits of the skyline.

"It looks like fire. A big one." Aerick murmured to himself.

"It does," Maeze answered, still dumbfounded by what he was seeing. They stared for a few minutes more, until full dark was fast approaching. The chorus of frogs began to sound and bugs zipping through the air. Briefly Maeze was distracted by the idea of catching a few of the green amphibians for a late snack when they reached the Fortress and home, but his better sense got the best of him. Practicality won out. They had to get back to the safety of the walls.

"We need to go now," Maeze said firmly and finally managed to tug his impetuous partner back to his seat and the oars. "Let's move."

Aerick rowed with energy once he was seated and realized how truly dark it was growing. Fearfully he flicked his gaze around at every bubble of sulfur and each ripple of fish that they passed in the boat. Maeze kept a sharp eye out as well. He did not care to be caught in a fight with Banelings in the dark. He shuddered at the idea of such a nightmarish encounter.

"What do you think the light on the horizon was," Aerick asked as they approached the safety of home. Some hours had passed in tense silence as each of them had pondered the strange sight on the horizon, and at the same time kept a vigil watch of their surroundings for any hint of danger. Now with the Fortress walls looming out of the dark in front of them, Maeze's partner finally seemed to loosen up.

"Not sure really," Maeze answered. "But it definitely looked like a fire. The longer I think on it the more certain I am. That was a fire."

"But what was burning?"

Indeed Maeze thought silently in response to his friend's question. What had been burning? What was there to burn so brightly and powerfully in a wet, dank marsh, especially from so far away? He pondered the question as they docked the boat and tied it up, then clumped with soggy boots back through the gate and into the relative security of the Fortress.

What could have caused such a fire to be burning on the horizon? As he thought, the conclusion to which he came shook the very foundations of all that he had believed to be true. Yet with these stark realizations came a desperate hope. So faint was the hope that it was almost snuffed out by the fear that accompanied it. But, stirred inside by his musings, Maeze let the hope flutter and grow in his chest, until the spark increased to the blaze he had seen on the horizon. Decisions were made as he walked in the dim, torch lit night back to his room. Tomorrow was a new day and Maeze intended to do the unthinkable.

Chapter Five

"Nobody leaves," Aerick stated incredulously. "It's never been done. There's nothing else out there. The Fortress is all there is."

"Listen to yourself," Maeze implored his friend in the dark haze of the hours between midnight and sunrise. He had stopped by his friend's rented room in the west quarter before they were to set out for their last day of hunting for the week. "We just witnessed a fire on the horizon, and it must have been enormous for us to see from such a distance. There has to be something else out there. Think, Aerick."

"We don't know whether the fire had anything to do with people, or a city, or anything. Lightning could have struck and set the swamp ablaze." Aerick pressed stubbornly, not willing to concede yet.

"The swamp? Ablaze? Really?" Maeze replied skeptically. "Name one time when lightning has ever set anything on fire that wasn't in this city. The surrounding landscape is too wet to burn. Only manmade buildings become dry enough for flames to catch."

Maeze directed his steady gaze at his friend. He tilted his head in a nonverbal repetition of his question to his partner. Maeze wanted company. He wanted Aerick to go with him. It would be easier to leave the docks if they looked like a pair of Slayers going out for their usual activities. It would also be safer on the journey with an extra set of hands to defend themselves should the need arise. And the need was almost definitely bound to arise; Banelings were everywhere. But the truth was, Maeze would go with or without Aerick. He was done with this place, this life. The reward of something new, a better life, was worth the risk of leaving.

He shook the small bag of supplies he had gathered discreetly, trying to entice his partner. By spending all of his saved coppers and trading a few extra tunics and a pair of socks, he had managed to get them enough supplies to last a few days. Hopefully, the journey wouldn't be longer than he had planned for.

"Well?" he asked his partner again.

"Nobody has ever gone more than a day's journey out from the Fortress. Anyone can see there isn't anything but endless marsh. No land, no islands, definitely no cities. All there is out there are reeds, fish, and Banelings." He shuddered. "I, for one, don't feel particularly like dying today, and what you're proposing is a suicide venture." Aerick was wavering a bit, Maeze could tell by his expression, but his words were still a resounding no. He tried another tactic.

"Quotas have already gone up to twenty Banelings per pair per week in the last few days. They're bound to rise again. The Grand Investigator will see to that, mark my words." Maeze spoke to his friend honestly. "How long do you expect to survive as a Slayer when the Death Tax rises to thirty or forty of the water devils per week? How many Ritual Woundings will you endure, just on the off chance you'll make it home to your bed that night, only to repeat the process the following day?" Maeze spoke from the heart, from all the bitterness he had felt these last three years.

Aerick's resolve was slipping. "Well," he hedged.

But Maeze continued over his attempt to speak. "The Grand Investigator doesn't care if he loses you. He's got his police thugs rounding up nearly every able bodied man in the west quarter to be thrown in jail and then added to the Slayers unit. Your death means nothing to him when he has an endless supply of replacements."

Maeze lifted up his tunic to reveal his own chest to Aerick. Four scars marked the part of his chest just above his heart. There were matching scars on his left hand as well, courtesy of the Binding ceremony when the Reader joined two Slayers together in partnership. The magic ritual was much like a marriage ceremony, the pair standing opposite each other with hands placed on the other's chest, just like a man and a woman. The only difference was blood. The Binding took place by a cut on the breast of one partner, and the other partner placed his cut hand over the wound, and vise versa, mingling their blood and their life energy into the forging of a partnership between Slayers. The Reader completed the rite. They grasped their weapons in hands smeared with their mixed blood and stuck the weapons into the forge, the Reader. It made them a pair, in effect creating them as Slayers, binding them together, to heal as the other killed. Without the ability to heal when their opposite killed Banelings, they were just men attempting to fight a losing battle. The magic made them more. The magic bound them in servitude to the Ruling Council but it made them more.

"You see these scars, Aerick?" Aerick's eyes trailed to his partner's chest. He only had one set of scars, as Maeze was his first partner. Maeze went on, "Three partners before you, and do you think anybody shed a tear for them when the Banelings dragged them under the dark curtain of water to the marshy depths to death? No. The Grand Investigator laughed and said they'd find a new replacement for me within the next two days." Maeze was furious now. All the hurt and anger of the last few years, of his whole life really, boiled over.

He spoke on, his rage fueling his words. "Well, I've had it, Aerick. I'm done with them, with this place, this Fortress, with this life. I'm going to risk my life one more time, but this time I'll do it for me. I'll risk my life once more for a purpose, on the off chance that maybe, just maybe," he emphasized his words by pausing slightly and dramatically lowering his voice, "there might be a better place, a better future out there for me somewhere."

"Do you really think they'll raise the Death Tax to forty per week?" Aerick asked in a small, frightened voice, reminding Maeze how young he was, only twenty years of age.

"I don't know, my friend. But I'm not staying to find out. The fire we saw might have been just a natural disaster and maybe I'll sail away into nothingness and die a horrible death in the marsh. But," he cocked his head and smiled, trying to inspire his friend, "maybe, I'll find a city. Perhaps there will be people, a place where there are no Slayers and I can make a new life. A real life."

His arguing done, he sat back to wait. He wanted Aerick to come along. The way things were going Maeze really did expect the Quotas to rise to at least thirty by the end of next week. The Grand Investigator was sadistic that way. It wouldn't be long before Slayers began dying at an even faster rate than they had been previously. He believed it was in his friend's best interest to accompany him. Yet, Maeze wanted a willing companion, not a tricked or coerced one.

He sat on the dirt floor of his friend's room, watching the flicker of emotions play across Aerick's face. The young Slayer was impulsive and his feelings flashed one then the next; fear, anxiety, hope, worry, then hope again. Finally, hope seemed to win out and he smiled a boyish smile.

"I don't really have anything keeping me here I guess. Ma died last year and Pa the year before. Don't have a gal or any sisters or brothers. All I really have is you, and if you're going, then I guess I am too," Aerick finished with a firm, confident grin now. "Ready?"

Maeze smiled as well. "Yes, I believe I am." His partner's commitment touched him deeply. They really were friends. It had been a long time since Maeze had been able to legitimately consider someone other than Merryweather a friend. It felt good.

They set out through the early morning dimness, the light of dawn not yet having pierced the skies. The alleys and streets of the Fortress were in a strangely quiet, early morning, moment. The street vendors from late the night before had only just packed up and gone home, while the early morning vendors had not quite made it to the streets yet. The stillness was potent for some reason. The air felt pregnant with possibility.

They were really doing it.

Maeze was really going to leave this place behind. The familiar anxiety and nervousness, the fear he felt in his gut as he approached his daily duties as a Slayer walking to the docks was still there, as always. But today there was something else. Maeze didn't know what lay ahead. Death maybe, but then, that wasn't really any different than an average day. However, the possibility of a future, his hope for something new, gave him a sense of excitement he had never before felt. The sense of anticipation he felt as he and Aerick made their way through the south quarter on their way to the docks was altogether foreign.

Lost in his thoughts, Maeze was hardly aware of the company of soldiers until Aerick tapped his shoulder nervously. Maeze blinked and looked up from his feet and the street in front of him.

Five men had arrayed themselves before them, blocking their path. To Maeze's dismay and frustration the last person on earth he wished to see was standing at their head, firmly planted in the dark alleyway in front of them.

The Grand Investigator smirked at them the way powerful men do when they believe weaker men are in their grasp for the toying. "What do we have here?" The thick bodied man in fine clothing asked. His hammy fingers idly tapped the sword at his hip in silent threat.

Maeze didn't answer, not knowing exactly what to say. Aerick followed suit, taking his cue from his older partner. The Grand Investigator stepped toward them and his men followed.

"Is this how you treat your betters, Slayer, by not answering them? I believe you owe me an answer." The official's face was ugly in his pleasure at toying with them the way a cat would mice.

"What do you want me to say?" Maeze inquired in frustration, no longer quite able to keep his tone respectful. He was leaving today, forever. He shouldn't have to deal with this power-monger now. "After all, you didn't really ask me much of a question. It's rather stupid really, because you know exactly who we are and what we do." Aerick glanced nervously at Maeze as he responded with discourtesy.

The Grand Investigator's face was red with anger now at being embarrassed in front of his men. He altered his tactics. "What's the sack on your back for? Stolen goods no doubt," he said viciously, looking for any excuse to punish Maeze.

Maeze was a bit nervous now. The sack was full of the supplies he had gathered. It was the only evidence that something odd was afoot. He had to direct the attention away. "Just a bit of food for the day's duties, Sir." He tried to make his voice as polite as possible again, cursing himself for his lack of self-control and his earlier insolent statement. Couldn't he have just kept his mouth shut until they were safely away? Maeze silently berated himself for his own rashness.

But the damage had already been done. The Grand Investigator took another step closer and then another, an evil grin on his face. His men followed, staring grimly at the two Slayers.

The official answered in a voice that said he was pleased with himself. "Oh, I think I'll need to verify the truth of your previous statement. Besides, your impertinence from a moment before has earned you a week in the cells and twenty lashes. I'll be administering the lashes myself."

The Grand Investigator was close enough now to reach for the bag. His hands came closer and Maeze knew it was all over. He couldn't talk his way out of this now, and he definitely didn't want to waste a week in a jail cell, not to mention the time spent recovering from the lashes. No, he was leaving today or he wasn't leaving at all.

In a split decision, Maeze ripped the flanged mace from his hip and brought it up in a powerful arch. Maeze wasn't much of a warrior really. He hadn't received any formal training, and even fighting the Banelings was more about desperation and flailing than any real technique. Yet the Grand Investigator was too close, and too surprised for Maeze to have any real trouble. Powerful bullies never seemed to believe that those they oppressed would ever actually stand up for themselves, so when the moment came they were caught unawares.

In the split second before Maeze's mace made contact, surprise, anger, and lastly fear danced across the Grand Investigator's face. Then Maeze's flanged mace cracked into the side of the official's head, ball crushing the skull and points jamming themselves deeply into his brain with a sickening crunch. Maeze fought the urge to throw up; he had never killed a man before. But the Grand Investigator was dead now and there was no turning back. Those thoughts flashed through his mind in an instant, before Maeze let the man drop and leapt at the shocked soldiers.

"Aerick!" he called in an urgent voice, and astoundingly the young man was right on his heels, the sword he carried jumping free of its sheath to slice open the belly of an unsuspecting guard. Two soldiers were down before they even had time to scream, one fell to Maeze's mace and the other to Aerick's sword. The last two were on guard now, but they appeared shocked and even afraid at the ferocity and unexpectedness of the two Slayers' attack, which had left their commander and two comrades dead in the filth of the alley.

Maeze advanced quickly on one of the soldiers. This had to be decided rapidly. It was still dark out, stars still twinkling in the sky. The Grand Investigator and his men had been off to an early start. Yet, Maeze didn't want to wait around for the city to awaken and discover the carnage in this alley.

He swung his mace and missed as the soldier dodged. The soldier made to jab him with his sword and now it was Maeze's turn to evade. He side stepped the thrust and then smashed the wrist holding the sword with his mace. Flanges bit deep into the soldier's arm and he screamed, piercing the darkness loudly. He dropped the blade convulsively and Maeze brought the full force of his mace to bear on the man's face, leaving a bloody dent where his nose had been. Aerick had finished off his soldier as well and the bodies hit the damp alley with a bloody splat.

"Quickly, let's roll the bodies face down in the gutter against the side of the building. Hopefully, it will be a few hours before anyone takes care to check them. We must be gone from here. Now." Maeze stooped to pick up the bag of food that he had dropped at the start of the fight and then he and Aerick lumbered the bodies onto their faces in the gutter. Evidence disposed of as well as possible, they set out at a run. They both felt the urgency to get away from the death scene.

"You killed the Grand Investigator!" Aerick murmured as they ran with a pale face. "He's on the Ruling Council. You'd hang or worse for what you did."

"Well then," Maeze replied solemnly, "it's a good thing we aren't planning to come back. Isn't it?" Aerick nodded in shock.

They reached the south gate to the Slayers' docks and the guard let them through without any questions. The sky was starting to grey with the coming of dawn, but the world was still not quite light yet. They picked the most water-worthy craft they could find and untied it. In the skiff they pushed off and Aerick, as usual, manned the oars with the strength of youth. They rowed out of the small harbor on the south side of the Fortress.

"West." Maeze directed, although Aerick already knew their course. He said it more to have something to say. The events of the last hour tumbled in on him. His excitement and anticipation of before had been replaced by adrenaline and the sense of urgency to make their getaway clean and quickly before anyone noticed the bodies in the alley.

"I thought for certain the guard at the dock gate would notice the fresh blood on your mace and ask questions," Aerick said in a relieved voice as they caught a small bog swirl and the current of the marsh pulled them westward through the ever-changing maze of floating islands of vegetation, reeds, and rushes.

Maeze nodded. He actually hadn't thought to worry about the blood on his weapon, but was glad it had not caused any trouble. "Too dark to see I guess. Or maybe the guard was still tired and not paying attention." Maeze answered the question as the dawn broke. They sailed on the small skiff westward, and the light of dawn painted the horizon behind them a bright grey haze. Maeze looked at the Fortress for the last time, a dark, grim silhouette against the light skyline. He would never return and the realization lent a lightness to his emotions. For good or for ill, this was the beginning of something new. Everything was going to change now.

They rowed steadily west, keeping a sharper pace than normal. Neither Aerick nor Maeze wanted to encounter any Banelings today, in contrast to a normal day spent waiting for and needing the fearful moment when they would be able to kill to meet the Quota. They took turns at the oars, and they made good time as the skiff sucked into a strong westerly bog swirl, a steady current that pulled them away from the home, the life they had known at the Fortress behind them.

They passed by small floating islands of vegetation, some covered with wild grains and free growing beans. The Ruling Council sent people out into the surrounding marshland to cultivate a few of the more permanent solid-ground islets, but this far away from the Fortress, it was all wild. Maeze thought of stopping to harvest some, but the current had them in such a steady westward trajectory that he was loathe to interrupt their progress. Something inside him itched to cover as much distance as possible. They kept a keen eye out for Banelings as they sailed, but both Aerick and Maeze were firmly focused on one thing—the journey west.

The first day passed uneventfully and night began to fall. "I've never heard of anybody going this far, a full day's journey out," Aerick said in a whisper.

"We'll be fine. We just need to find a solid piece of ground to rest for the night. Then we'll set out in the morning again at first light," Maeze answered pragmatically.

"What if Banelings come?" Aerick was frightened, Maeze could tell. Well, truth be told, so was Maeze. This was the unknown. Nobody liked the prospect of a night spent in the marsh. Maeze had certainly done everything in his power to avoid it his entire life.

He breathed in deeply then answered honestly. "If they come, we fight," he said to his young friend. "And most likely, we'll die. So pray to the Forgotten Gods that they don't take notice of our passage."

Aerick swallowed hard, but then nodded resolutely. They kept an eye out in the fading light, until, in the middle of a particularly thick series of rushes taller than a man's head while standing in a boat, they saw firm ground. They pulled the boat up and Aerick hopped out to stomp his boots on the soggy ground while Maeze moored the craft.

"Seems firm enough." Aerick smiled as he looked at Maeze. He stomped again in the muck to prove his point. The land was indeed firmly rooted and not floating, even if it was very moist.

Maeze nodded agreeably. "Looks like a good enough spot. I'm hungry and I could use some food. Let's pull the boat up as far onto the land as possible. The firm ground was only a space of mud about five by ten feet jutting up from the marsh. Small but sheltered by the rushes, it was a perfect place to spend the night, if one didn't mind being damp. They dragged the boat up onto the land and ended up sitting in the boat to avoid the worst of the mud. It wasn't particularly comfortable, but then, Maeze had never expected this to be a comfortable trip.

"Beans?" Maeze pulled a jar of already baked beans out of his sack of provisions. The beans were cold and they didn't have the means or the desire to start a fire. It didn't seem advisable to start a fire and light a beacon at their location for any passing Baneling— so they ate the food the way it was, right from the jar. They passed the dirty, glass jar back and forth, scooping out meager handfuls of the food with their fingers since, in his haste to get ready, Maeze had forgotten utensils of any kind. Finishing the jar and then wiping their fingers clean on their breeches, they settled in for a chill night under the stars.

"I've never spent the night in the marsh," Aerick murmured sleepily, "never really seen much of the night sky except from within the confines of the Fortress." Most Slayers were back by the time sunset arrived since it was not advisable at all to be out in the swamp in the dark. Aerick continued to talk. "It's rather pretty, isn't it? All the twinkling stars. It's hard to see those stars in the city with the lights of torches and every other distraction to take your mind off the sky."

Maeze grunted his assent. He wasn't really one for idle chatter. "Let's be quiet now. We want our night to be as silent and uneventful as possible."

Aerick agreed fervently and situated himself on one of the benches in the boat, his arms crossed and fingers tucked underneath the arms to keep them warm. He looked very young all of a sudden, and Maeze felt a sense of responsibility for him that he had never before experienced. Aerick was in this because of him. He had to make sure to keep him safe.

"I'll take first watch. I'll wake you when it's your turn," Maeze said to his partner.

"Alright," Aerick said almost in a drowse. "Do you think anybody followed us? Will we be chased?"

"No. Nobody knows that we killed the soldiers and the Grand Investigator because there were no witnesses. So when our boat doesn't check in by nightfall, they'll assume we're just two more Slayers lost to the war of attrition with these cursed fens." But Aerick was already asleep, exhausted from a full day spent rowing. Maeze sat up half the night, keeping an eye on their surroundings, but nothing stirred, not even the rushes in a nighttime breeze. When he could keep his eyes open no longer, he woke Aerick and took his turn for rest.

The morning light was bright as it peeked over the tops of the reeds and rushes surrounding their tiny haven from the water. Aerick had drifted off to sleep at some point and morning had come. They had survived their first night in the swamp. Maeze thanked the Forgotten Gods and hoped against hope they wouldn't need to spend another such night in the marsh to test their good fortune. How far away had the mysterious fire been the evening before last? It had been a strange occurrence, distinguishable by its novelty, yet so faint as to be easy to miss. Only chance had brought it to their attention. Was it two days journey, three? Longer? Maeze wished it would be a short trip. Something told him that their luck at seeing not a single Baneling yesterday or last night would not last.

They pushed the boat off the mucky bit of firm land and set the prow west with the rising sun to their backs. The marsh was a strange sight in early morning. Wisps of mist danced lightly on the water, shooting upwards in odd streams as if yanked up by some unseen current of air only to drop back low again a few feet farther on. The mist was thin and easy to see through. It didn't obscure the vision, rather making the world appear a shimmering sheen of grey, water droplets before the warm, morning sun burned it away.

They rowed onwards, westwards all day, eating as they sailed, seeing nothing living except for nature. A few fish rippled the calm surface of the marsh and Maeze was only moderately tempted to catch one. They had enough supplies for a few more days and he hoped they wouldn't need more than that. After all, if he had been able to see the fire the other night, it would have to be close enough to reach, right? Other than the fish, there was the occasional stilt legged waterfowl, stretching their beaks down from a floating blob of weeds and muck to try and catch the silver flashes of minnows. There were also a swarm of gnats and mosquitos following them and dragonflies aplenty buzzing all over. But no sign of Banelings. And more disturbingly, nothing on the westward horizon to imply that anything human or manmade lay ahead. Maeze began to worry. He told himself it took lots of time to cover distance in an environment so marshy and mucky as this, that they would arrive at their destination soon. But nothing arose to confirm those internal encouragements.

The next night passed in similar fashion. They found a small hummock of land— this time it actually was dry, not just solid and muddy—and they were able to sleep out of the boat. The night passed again without incident and they woke up the next morning to begin their third day of the journey.

"Today's the day, eh?" Aerick said with a forced brightness. He seemed to pick up on Maeze's anxiety and was using his usual optimism to lighten the mood.

"I hope so, Aerick. I hope so."

"It has to be, doesn't it? I mean after all, I don't think we could have seen something burning from farther away than the distance we'll cover today," Aerick said, now looking to Maeze for agreement. "Right?"

Maeze nodded soberly. "Right." What his young friend was carefully avoiding was the frightening prospect of Maeze having made a mistake, the idea that somehow Maeze had been confused several evenings ago when he saw the glow on the horizon. What if Aerick had been right, and it had been lightning or who knew what else? Maeze certainly didn't claim to know overly much about the world around them. Could something unbeknownst to him have caused such a glow? The question was a burr in his mind and he couldn't shake the worry. The expectancy and hope he had felt at the start of the journey had faded, leaving only a vague remnant of its presence, greatly overshadowed by the anxiety and fear of this all being for nothing. The fear that their fight and escape and everything was wasted.

"Don't even think it," Aerick said with an uncharacteristically knowing look in his eyes. "Just don't."

"What?"

"I know you, Maeze. You are second guessing yourself. We had to do this. The day we left was Quota day. We were fifteen Banelings short of the Death Tax and odds were, we wouldn't likely have survived the day."

It was true, Maeze nodded his agreement silently. The young man was right, they likely would already be dead right now had they stayed, what with the way things were trending in regards to Slayers, but that knowledge didn't make the worry any easier. Maeze wanted so badly for there to be something at the end of this quest. Hopelessness began sinking its dirty fingers into his heart.

They rowed onwards through midmorning. The sunlight glancing off the water hitting their faces with its light until they both gained a pinkish cast from the heat and the reflections. Mud was a good cover for days like today, you could smear it on and protect yourself. It was also a decent salve afterwards, cool and moist to comfort skin ravaged by the hot sun. It didn't smell nice though.

He did his best to release his fears and worries from before. Maeze's thoughts drifted as they traveled, and he assumed Aerick was lost in thought as well, since they didn't speak. They just sat in companionable silence as they rowed and Maeze found himself rather enjoying being out in the world with his friend, with no agenda to fight or to kill, just the journey ahead and the prospect of a happy future.

It happened suddenly and there was nothing Maeze could do to stop it.

Lost in his idle thoughts about the sun and mud and healing concoctions, Maeze watched in absolute horror as a clammy white hand shot up out of the water beside the gently coasting boat and yanked Aerick over the side of the boat and into the water. A clear, thin claw on the forefinger of the Baneling's hand jammed tip first into Aerick's throat and Maeze could see the blood spurt out over its pale, spindly, webbed fingers, as it cupped the red flow to its mouth to drink its fill.

"No!" Maeze shouted in anguish as he watched his friend drift listlessly next to the boat. Aerick was choking on whatever he was attempting to say, not able to get the words past his blood clogged throat.

In a flash Maeze was at the side of the boat. He saw the red film begin to creep up to cover the milky eyes of the Baneling and he saw the red color also begin to fill the single claws on the thing's forefingers. If the transformation were completed, Maeze would have no chance. A Baneling in a blood frenzy was entirely too powerful for one man to defeat. He lashed out with his mace, flanges biting deep into the Baneling's eyes, the metal ball of his weapon cracking the head open. He ripped his weapon free and swung again and again until he saw the life fade from the beast's eyes.

Turning, Maeze saw the body of his friend drifting downwards almost submerged now in the muddy brown waters of the marsh. Frantically he pulled Aerick back into the boat, hoping, praying that killing the Baneling had been enough to heal his friend. He knew it wouldn't be. A slit throat couldn't be healed by one Baneling death, even with the Slayer bond. What good was magic, the Binding, if it couldn't save the one person you wanted it to? Why did it have to fail him now of all times? He thought bitterly.

Cradling Aerick to his chest he watched the blood flow from his partner's neck. It coursed slightly less forcefully from his throat than a moment ago, with some healing having taken place by way of their bond as Slayers. However, it was clear the wound had not been aided enough by the solitary creature's death to truly stop. Crying, Maeze tried to plug his hand over the flow, but it was no use, it seeped out from the cracks in his fingers and underneath and around the sides of his hands until he saw the life fade from his friend's eyes, much as it had from the Baneling's a few minutes earlier.

Realizing he was sobbing now, Maeze clutched the only true friend he'd had in years to his chest, rocking him back and forth.

"Why?" he muttered fiercely. "Why did you have to go and die on me? Why now? I was supposed to keep you safe."

There was no response. Maeze wasn't surprised for he had expected none. He didn't know how long he sat there before the facts began to weigh on him. It might have been seconds, minutes, or even hours, but eventually his practical side awakened from his grief. Aerick's blood was in the water and it would likely attract more Banelings. He needed to be long gone from this spot before they arrived en masse. Aerick's death could not be allowed to go for nothing. Maeze would press on until he reached his destination—what that was he did not know, or even if it existed—or until he could go no further.

Unable to bear letting his friend's body sink into the sinister mire of the marsh, Maeze kept his friend in the boat. He grabbed the oars, relieved they had been locked into the oarlocks when the attack had happened, and then resumed the course westward. Tears still trickled down his cheeks. It was strange to miss somebody. He hadn't missed anyone since his mother had died, many long years ago. With not one of his partners had he allowed himself to develop a closer relationship than what was strictly a professional partnership, just two men working a job. Yet Aerick had somehow wormed his way into Maeze's life, into his heart. With his optimism, impulsiveness, and youthful exuberance Aerick had become the friend that Maeze hadn't known he'd needed. And now he was gone. Maeze even realized he would miss his friend's indecisiveness and inability to hold an opinion—it had always been easy for anybody to convince Aerick of a point of view. Yet those qualities had made him who he was and Maeze mourned for him as he rowed.

With a determination and grit he didn't know he had within him, Maeze rowed. His steady strokes ate up the distance, the expanse of murky water before his boat, until the twilight began to fall. The wisps of mist began to reappear, twirling on the water. But they did not stay, a breeze banished them, stirring with it the fetid reek of the fens. It was all a blur to Maeze who rowed west in a stupor of pain and anguish, a haze of grief. He cried again, and he hardly looked ahead at where he was rowing other than in a general sense to make sure to keep the setting sun, the westward mark, before him.

Gradually Maeze began to regain attentiveness. Suddenly, he realized the horizon looked different. The sun had sunk beneath the skyline before him until only a fading light was still illuminating the world, but something was off. The horizon ahead of Maeze was much too large, too bulky and high above the water. That horizon couldn't be rushes, could it? Reeds and rushes didn't grow that big. He paddled onwards as the night fell. As the darkness came, the dark shape of the horizon still blotted out the stars. It looked like an island many times the size of the one he had left. Eventually, he came to his conclusion. It had to be. There was no other explanation. The horizon ahead of him was land.

Maeze had never seen land higher than a few feet out of the marsh. Even the land of the lone, big island upon which the Fortress had been built, had no rise. The wall of the Fortress was the highest he had ever been in his entire life. Yet, the bulky shape of land growing ever closer was much higher than the highest tower of the wall. Many times higher.

Then Maeze noticed off to his left a faint glow, emitting a weak light. He turned the prow of his boat and continued rowing southwest now.

"We're almost there, Aerick," he said to his dead friend in the boat with him. "I don't really have any idea where *there* is, but it's not where we came from. It's different." He knew it was silly to speak so to the dead, maybe it meant he'd gone crazy, but he wanted to share this with someone. There was something other than the Fortress. Nobody, not even the Ruling Council, knew of the existence of anything notable outside a half-day's distance from the walls of the city. Yet here he was, ending his third day of travel and he was someplace *new*.

As he drew closer to the faint glow, the shape of a harbor loomed up out of the darkness ahead of him. Closer and closer his craft crept as he pulled the oars until he was in the harbor of a city, a city ten times bigger than the Fortress.

He pulled up to the quay, his boat knocking against the stone docks of this foreign city. The city had an enormous wall, broken in some places, blackened from fire. The buildings of the city were taller than the wall, mansions rose up in architectural masterpieces, palaces, apartments. Spires twisted their way towards the midnight sky, torches lighting the scene for him to see.

A guard—at least Maeze supposed he was a guard since he carried a spear and wore armor—approached. "Who goes there? Who gave you authorization to take your craft out? Nobody is supposed to leave the harbor for personal reasons until the surrounding area has been surveyed and deemed safe."

"I…I'm not from here," Maeze said faltering slightly. What did one say at a time like this? "I don't know anything of your rules or even where I am."

"Who's this in the boat? How did he die?" the guard asked dangerously.

"Baneling," Maeze answered softly, sadly.

"Marshbanes killed him?" The guard lessened his firm resolve and seemed to recognize something different was going on here. "I am sorry. That's why we've locked down all watercraft for the time being. It's not safe out there right now. We haven't had an assault like this for nearly a century. The bastards came in waves and droves."

"Where am I exactly?" Maeze questioned.

"What do you mean?" The guard asked curiously. "This is Farstenhold. Don't you live here?"

"No, I'm not from here."

"Where are you from?" The guard asked slowly, lowering his spear in his curiosity.

"I'm from elsewhere." Maeze pointed behind him, indicating the marsh and the many miles stretching eastward that led towards the Fortress.

"But nothing lives in the marsh," the guard said incredulously. He was very perplexed now. "Farstenhold is the most eastern city in Orstantian. This city helps protect the people and towns inland from the dangers of the wild. There have been numerous expeditions sent out in all directions in the swamp and none of them ever came back. Over the years we assumed nothing lived out there. Except the bastards," he added with a vile curse. "Marshbanes control everything east of here."

"Well, you have part true. Banelings—Marshbanes as you call them—pretty much have the run of things where I come from," Maeze answered tiredly but agreeably. He didn't want to get on the bad side of the first person he met in wherever this place was. Was it Orstantian the guard had called it? Or maybe Farsten-something? Or both? Maeze was quickly growing too tired to think clearly.

Two more soldiers walked up the dock to see what the fuss was all about. The guard Maeze had been talking with spoke up. "Sir, this man says he's from, well the marsh I guess, and he's just arrived."

One of the approaching soldiers nodded. He must be the captain. "I guess I've heard of stranger things happening but not many."

The first guard spoke again. "Maybe he..." he paused and looked at Maeze, "What's your name?"

"Maeze."

"Maybe Maeze, here, could go to the barrack and get a hot meal and clean pallet for the night. He looks exhausted," the first guard concluded.

The captain nodded his agreement then spoke to the soldier who had arrived with him. "Soldier Kanel. Would you be so kind as to escort this refugee to the barracks where he can rest and recover? Also, please send a detail of men to come out here to collect this man's friend and give him a proper burial."

Maeze said his thanks and walked away with the second

soldier while the captain stayed to have a few more words with the first guard who had stopped Maeze initially. Maeze looked back with regret at the body of Aerick. At least he would get a proper burial instead of being dumped in the swamp like the bodies back at the Fortress, at least he would get that much dignity. A lone tear trickled down Maeze's cheek as he walked, trying to keep pace with the soldier.

As sad as he was about the death of his friend, he couldn't quell the sense of wonder he felt as he walked through the gate into the city. He was actually in a place inhabited by humans, a place far away from the Fortress. A city that, from what he understood, was part of a much larger region. It was almost too much to comprehend.

"Do you have Slayers?" Maeze asked.

"What? What's that? Soldiers you mean?" the soldier grunted in answer.

Maeze decided to try it from a different perspective. "What do you do with criminals here?"

"Why they go to jail, obviously." The soldier seemed annoyed by Maeze's strange questions.

Maeze pressed a bit further. "Is the law fair here?"

"Fair, why of course it's fair! The King's a good man. Looks out for his people. Pays us soldiers well too."

The second soldier seemed a surly sort and didn't speak much after that. But Maeze was fine with the silence. He already had his answer. Not once in his life had he ever heard a commoner stick up for the Ruling Council or the upper class of the Fortress with such verve. This place was different, Maeze could tell.

Maeze walked with him. In the dark he could see the burnt out husks of buildings everywhere. It looked as if the entire city had been ablaze at some point. Indeed, there were still sections of the city where the embers of said fire had not yet burned out. Likely those embers were the glow that had caught his eye tonight.

"What happened here?" Maeze asked the soldier as they walked.

"Invasion of Marshbanes of epic proportions. We haven't had an attack like this in a century." The soldier grunted. "Thousands upon thousands of them attacked a few days back. We killed them by the hundreds but many reached blood frenzy." He paused and looked at Maeze. "You know what blood frenzy means?"

Maeze nodded affirmatively.

The soldier continued. "Hundreds of them, maybe thousands, reached the frenzy and breached the wall. They tore the city apart, killed more people than I can count and knocked torches over in the weapons storehouses, setting the naphtha and pitch on fire. Other Marshbanes knocked over torches in other sections of Farstenhold and before you knew what had happened, the entire city was burning. I've never seen such a sight. It took us days to put the worst of it out."

So that was what the glow on the horizon had been days ago. Farstenhold had been burning, so completely ablaze that the brilliance had shined for miles.

Even though it was the middle of the night, people worked everywhere to put the city to right. There were people lugging away parts of the burned shells of houses and buildings, people scrubbing the charred stone walls of cathedrals, there were even people washing the streets.

"Place looks a mess, don't it?" The soldier spat as he asked the question disdainfully. "Not a pretty sight, eh? Certain parts of the city are still burning. There and there," he pointed out the embers of fire still glowing with heat in front of dutiful water workers. "But we survived, didn't we? And we took all those slimy bastards to the grave. They won't be bothering us for years." The soldier looked moderately pleased with that.

"On the contrary," Maeze disagreed, "I find this to be the most spectacular thing I've ever seen." And he meant it. Maeze again felt the hope, which had sparked this entire venture, blossom up inside him. He closed his eyes and breathed in the burnt fragrance of a new life.

The guard looked at him strangely but decided not to respond. Maeze looked at the remnants of the blaze, the coals and embers clinging to existence in different sections of the city. They were all the last vestiges of the giant blaze, the signal fire that had called him here. The city might still be burning, but it was beautiful. It was a beacon of light, of hope. *Burning hope*.

Fate had given Maeze a second chance at life.

About the Author

Mathias Colwell grew up in far Northern California exploring redwood forests and cloudy beaches. He loves God, his family, and friends. Mathias has been a writer for most of his life, drafting his first stories as young as eight years of age. His desire to write fantasy was inspired by such authors as J.R.R. Tolkien, David Eddings and the late Robert Jordan. He is an avid traveler and all-around adventurer, having visited or lived in 27 countries. His travels have led him around the world to five continents including stays in Siberia, Spain, and Chile, and he attributes many of his passions and goals in life to these experiences. In his free time he enjoys reading, outdoor activities such as soccer, snowboarding and water sports. Mathias has a passion for issues pertaining to social justice and human rights and hopes to influence these areas in the future.

Other Works by the author at Melange, Fire and Ice for Young Adults

An Age of Mist
The Collector